TROUBLED WATERS

TROUBLED WATERS

Claire Lorrimer

This first world edition published in Great Britain 2004 by
SEVERN HOUSE PUBLISHERS LTD of
9–15 High Street, Sutton, Surrey SM1 1DF.
Originally published 1961 in Great Britain under the title
Last Chance by *Patricia Robins*. Fully revised and updated
by the author, reset and retitled for this Severn House edition.
This first world edition published in the USA 2004 by
SEVERN HOUSE PUBLISHERS INC of
595 Madison Avenue, New York, N.Y. 10022.

British Library Cataloguing in Publication Data

Lorrimer, Claire
    Troubled waters
    1. Adult children living with parents - Scotland - Glasgow - Fiction
    2. Romantic suspense novels
    I. Title
    823.9'14 [F]

    ISBN 0-7278-6123--9

Typeset by Palimpsest Book Production Ltd.,
Polmont, Stirlingshire, Scotland.
Printed and bound in Great Britain by
MPG Books Ltd., Bodmin, Cornwall.

One

Bob stood in the porch, his arms round Alison's shoulders, his face against her soft, red-gold hair.

'Couldn't you come with me, darling?' he asked. 'It's sure to be a good do and I won't feel like going without you.'

Alison withdrew from the comforting presence of his arms and shivered slightly in the night air. They had just come home from their weekly night out together.

'I wish I could, Bob. But I don't think Mrs Cuthbert will come on a Wednesday because of her children. I can't leave Mother alone, you know that!'

'I suppose so,' Bob said, disappointment and uncertainty mixed in the tone of his voice. 'Though sometimes I wonder if Mrs Craig wouldn't be all right on her own. After all, we don't have to go till about nine and by then she'd have had her tea and gone to bed.'

'But suppose she has one of her attacks?'

It was always the same, Bob thought. In many ways, the unselfish part of Alison's nature, which was one of the many reasons he loved her, was also their undoing. They could go out only once a week when a neighbour came in to sit with Alison's mother, and once a week for a few hours isn't much when you wanted to spend all your spare time with the girl you loved. And there just did not seem to be any hope on the horizon that things would improve.

Ever since Mr Craig had died suddenly and unexpectedly from a heart attack, Mrs Craig had lost her own good health. She had painful attacks of arthritis and spent more time in

1

bed than out of it. Of course, it was three years now since Alison's father had departed. Alison had been seventeen at the time and just about to start at Glasgow University, but of course she'd given up the idea of becoming a teacher and had left school to start work in a biscuit factory. Someone had to replace her father as the breadwinner and there wasn't anyone else when Mrs Craig collapsed.

'Dr McFaddon says she'll get well again soon,' Alison had told Bob. 'He says the shock started it, and of course she isn't young, like your mother, Bob.'

He'd gone on to university without Alison and had quite a good job now as an engineer just outside Glasgow. He was earning good money and there was really no reason why he and Alison shouldn't be married – except that so far Alison wouldn't consent even to an engagement.

'Do you honestly love me?' he asked now, drawing her back into his arms. '*Really?*'

'Of course I do!' Alison cried. 'You know there's never been anyone else in my life . . . not since I was fourteen and first saw you. Whyever should you doubt it?'

It was on the tip of his tongue to tell her that her love and care for her mother so outweighed everything else that it left no room for loving him, but the words seemed childish and resentful and he didn't want to add to her burdens by accusing her of neglecting him. Old Mrs Craig made enough demands on her time and attention.

'Well, you'd better be getting in, I suppose,' he said doubtfully, unwilling to let her go but somehow feeling the futility of trying to keep her there on her doorstep.

'Good night, Bob dear, and thanks for a lovely evening,' Alison said, reaching up to receive his last goodnight kiss. 'I'm sorry about Wednesday – the dance, I mean. I will ask Mrs Cuthbert but I daren't hold out too much hope.'

She went indoors and trod softly across the carpeted hall, knowing her way in the darkness. But quiet as she was, Mrs Craig heard her and called down:

'That you, Alison?'

'Yes, Mother. I was just going to make a hot drink.'

2

'Bring it up here, dear, and tell me about your evening. I can't sleep, anyway.'

Alison went into the kitchen and stood by the old gas cooker watching the milk as it heated. She felt unaccountably depressed. What was wrong with her tonight? She didn't feel a bit like going into her mother's room as she usually did for a last little gossip. Somehow she wanted to be alone, to try to fathom out what was wrong between her and Bob. Of course, he was disappointed about the dance on Wednesday. But she really did mean to try to get Mrs Cuthbert. And if she couldn't? Maybe Mother wouldn't mind so much, just for a few hours, she thought. I'll ask her.

She couldn't get it out of her mind what Beryl James had said last week. Beryl, like herself, worked at the biscuit factory and although they were so very different in type they were still quite good friends.

'Take a tip from me, Alison, and keep a tighter rein on that young fellow of yours. I saw him in the pub last week with ever such a good-looking blonde.'

She'd just laughed at the time, but when she'd asked Bob about it, at first he'd denied he'd even been there. Then he admitted it.

'I don't know who she was, Alison, and that's the truth. I just picked her out of the crowd, you know the way all the fellows do who haven't got regular girls. It didn't mean a thing, honest. Besides, what harm is there? It wasn't as if I'd broken a date with you. I can't stay home every evening just because you have to!'

'I don't even expect you to,' Alison said truthfully. 'I asked you only out of curiosity. It was only when you said you hadn't been there at all that I began to wonder what had been going on. Besides,' she lifted her head proudly, 'I've no exclusive right to you any more than you have to me.'

That's why he'd kissed her more passionately than ever before – a kiss which had frightened and disturbed her.

'I'm in love with you, Alison, you and no one else. I've got to see more of you. Can't you possibly come to the dance with me on Wednesday?'

3

She would go. Bob wanted her to and it was time she tried to give him a little more attention. If only . . .

She mixed in the cocoa and carried the two cups up to her mother's room.

Mrs Craig was in her late fifties. She was still a nice-looking woman, grey-haired, with Alison's lovely green eyes. Only the strained, unhappy expression on her face spoiled the pleasant first impression one might otherwise have had. She eyed her daughter with a question behind the actual words:

'Enjoy yourself, darling?' What she was really thinking was: 'They haven't got engaged yet, have they? Alison wouldn't – not without telling me first.'

'Yes, thank you, Mother,' the girl said, putting down the tray and walking over to the curtained window. It wasn't a luxurious room but it was warm and comfortable. Mrs Craig spent a lot of time there.

'Mother!' Alison's voice was strained and the older woman looked at the slim young back anxiously. Was this the moment she so dreaded coming at last? 'Mother, Bob wants me to go to a dance on Wednesday. It's . . . it's rather important to him. And I'd like to go – that is if you wouldn't mind Mrs Cuthbert coming in.'

Mrs Craig leant back against her pillows, relaxing.

'Why, of course not, dear. Though I don't think Mrs Cuthbert will come. You know she said quite definitely she can manage only Saturdays.'

Alison turned suddenly and faced her mother, her eyes full of appeal.

'Mother, if she can't come, would you mind if . . . if I went all the same? I wouldn't be late and I could tuck you up first and see you had everything you wanted.'

Mrs Craig looked down at the hands folded in front of her on the sheet. Her mind was racing with questions. Alison had never suggested leaving her alone before. Was this a prelude to other evenings? Why was it so important to her and to Bob? Was an engagement in the wind after all? Not yet, she prayed silently; please not yet!

4

'It wouldn't be a regular thing,' Alison said in a tight, constrained voice, as if reading her mother's thought. 'Just this once, Mother?'

I mustn't be selfish, I really mustn't! the older woman told herself. Just once . . .

'All right, dear! I'm sure I'll be able to manage. Besides, I haven't had one of my attacks for quite a long while. Maybe I'm really getting better.'

Alison hurried over to the bed, her eyes shining now, her cheeks flushed.

'Thank you, Mother,' she said, bending to kiss the grey hair. 'I promise I won't be late back, and Bob says we needn't go till nine. I could ask him here for supper first, couldn't I? Then we can all three have a few hours together before we leave. You'd like that.'

'Yes, dear. You're a good girl and a wonderful comfort to me. I don't know what I whould have done after your father died if—'

'Mother, don't, please. You'll only upset yourself. And I don't do anything any other daughter wouldn't do. You can't help being ill.'

'It's such a strain on you, dear; I often think you ought to marry Bob and go away and lead your own life.'

'Mother, you know I'd never leave you, never! As for marrying Bob – well, one day, I suppose, we will marry. But it needn't be for a long time yet. We aren't even engaged.'

'But you are in love with each other?'

Alison flushed in sudden shyness.

'Yes, we are in love. There's never been anyone but Bob – you know that, Mother. But even if – when – we do marry, I shan't go away. Bob knows that. He wouldn't ask me to. You'd live with us. Let's not talk about it any more.'

'All right, dear.' Mrs Craig accepted the cup of cocoa, now cooled, and a moment later Alison rose and said she was going to bed.

In her own small bedroom, sparsely furnished and rather cold, she undressed as quickly as possible and climbed in between the sheets. Her spirits were high yet she felt

5

exhausted, as if she had been in a battle with her mother.

What a silly thing to think! she told herself sharply. Mother and I understand each other – we never row. I ought to have asked her before now if she'd mind my leaving her. Somehow it seems to have become the accepted thing over the years since Father died that I never would go out except on Saturdays. Father . . .

Her thoughts centred on the man who had once filled her life – a big jovial red-haired Scotsman who had laughed and joked and boomed his way through life, making friends but never money, loved by all who met him. He'd been the pivot round which they had revolved and Alison had adored him.

Perhaps it was just as well she'd had her mother to care for afterwards or she might have felt his sudden death much more keenly herself. As it was, with her mother completely collapsed from shock and grief, she had had no time for private sorrows. Suddenly all the responsibilities were on her shoulders. Mr Craig had left them nothing but debts, and by the time these were cleared by the sale of some of their better pieces of furniture, it was clear that she'd have to abandon the idea of going to university and get a job.

So the years had gone by, in retrospect, terribly fast. She was twenty-one – a woman now. And she felt older. It was only with other girls that she felt younger. They all seemed to be so much more sophisticated than she was. All the girls in the factory were either engaged or married. They led hectic lives, working all day, out nearly every night either at the cinema or dancing. Compared with them, Alison felt young and inexperienced and their gossip about their different experiences confused and embarrassed her. She always tried to avoid their confidences and mostly now they didn't discuss their private lives with her or near her. But they all liked her, believing her to be somehow different from them. They respected her, too, for the completely unselfish way she devoted herself to her invalid mother, even while, among themselves, they spoke of Mrs Craig as 'a selfish old besom!'

Alison loved her mother. Her love was always ringed with pity, for she realized that with the death of her father there

6

was nothing left in life to bring her mother happiness. She had vowed to herself on her eighteenth birthday that anything she could ever do to make her mother's life easier she would do it, no matter what the cost to herself.

It did not occur to Alison that she herself had set the pattern of their lives. Perhaps if Mrs Craig had had more to do immediately following her husband's death she would have got over the shock and pulled herself together. But there were no young children to force her out of her well of grief – only Alison, who already had taken up the reins and was running everything smoothly.

She sank back into her chasm of sorrow and allowed her daughter to plan as she wished. The more Alison did, the more she let her do. For beyond everything clse Alison was efficient. She ran the house, cleaned it, cooked, kept her job and cared for her mother without any seeming effort, and she never complained.

'I'm happy doing these things for you, Mother,' the girl had said, and Mrs Craig believed her.

But Alison couldn't sleep that night . . . couldn't, because her mind and heart were restless with a strange, new discontent. She ought to feel pleased. Bob would be happy about the dance on Wednesday. Her mother really had seemed better these last few weeks. Summer had come and they were having a lovely warm spell; there was even talk of the girls getting a rise at work – not much, but it would help. She might be able to put enough by to buy herself a new winter coat, for hers was the same one her mother had bought for her ready for university wear. It looked shabby, out of date and childish now.

What was unsettling her? Not her mother. Bob, perhaps? Was he falling out of love with her? He hadn't lingered very long tonight, the way he usually did, trying to detain her till the last possible moment before she left him. Would it be the end of the world if Bob did find himself another girl?

This is silly! Alison told herself sharply as she turned for the third time on her pillow. Bob is all I have to look forward to at the end of every day. My few hours with him are all

7

the fun, the excitement, the interest in my life.

She'd known Bob so long; he was as much part of her life as the four walls round her, comfortable, familiar, understanding, secure. During the immediate crisis after her father's death he'd helped her in every way he could; his parents, too. They'd even offered to lend Alison money, but much as they had needed it, Alison had refused. She was far too proud to be beholden to anyone.

Because her mother had been so broken up Alison had had to try to maintain a cheerful optimism in her presence. Alone with Bob she had found comfort in tears and it was then Bob had first told her he loved her.

Alison tried to think now of marriage. She could visualize Bob coming home from work, tired, pleased to see her; she could see herself bringing him his tea, cooking his favourite dishes. And when it came to the more intimate side of married life . . . strangely her mind shied away from such thoughts. Yet if they were married she could lie in a double bed with him, her body his to do with as he wished. He could make love to her 'properly' – the way he wanted. In a way, she wanted it, too, but not until after she was married.

She wondered sometimes if there were anything wrong with her. Sex was all most of the girls at the factory talked about. They seemed to know all about it, too. They accepted sex as a kind of appetite, necessary rather the way eating and drinking were necessary. But for her it had to be different. It had to be linked with love, a love so strong that she would want to give herself, all of herself for life. Why, when she loved Bob, did she not feel that way about him now? She did love him. It wasn't just his good looks. She liked his personality, his cheerfulness, his good temper, his outlook on life. He wasn't a prey to moods the way she was, up one minute and down in a trough of depression the next. She always knew where she stood with a boyfriend like Bob. Funny the way she still thought of him sometimes as a boy. He was a man, six foot tall and well built. He often played football for the local amateur team and lots of people said they thought he could have been a professional footballer if

8

he wished. But that would have wasted a good brain. He was doing well in engineering, too.

At long last Alison slept, her red-brown hair falling in soft curls against the white pillow, soot-black lashes curling down childishly over her cheeks. In sleep the lines of worry, anxiety and fatigue were wiped from her and she looked radiantly beautiful, a young woman on the threshold of life – and love.

Two

'**B**ob, I'm terribly sorry, but I shan't be able to come tonight after all.'

Alison gripped the telephone receiver in a hot, damp hand. The call-box seemed stifling this June afternoon. Bob's voice came back to her, distorted and unfamiliar over the headset.

'Alison, why not? You said on Monday—'

'I know. It's Mother. She had a terrible attack this morning. I was late for work. I can't leave her tonight. There'll be nothing done. I had to put her back to bed. It's such bad luck, Bob. She was feeling fine when she woke up and actually got up before me to go and make breakfast. She hasn't done that in years. Then, suddenly, just as I came downstairs, she collapsed. I called Dr McFaddon but he was out on a maternity case. He hadn't called when I rushed home at lunchtime. I'll have to go straight home after work, Bob. I'm terribly sorry – disappointed, too.'

She waited for Bob's reassuring voice, telling her it didn't matter all that much, that he understood. Instead, he said:

'It's not right, Alison. We'd both been looking forward to it so much. Can't you make it – *somehow*? I'd fixed for us to join two friends of mine and their girls. We'd all go in a party together.'

'Bob dear, I am sorry. I'm as disappointed as you are.'

'If you can't come, I shall have to call off for myself, too,' Bob said slowly. 'Can't make a five-some.'

'Couldn't you take Julie?' Alison asked. Julie was Bob's sixteen-year-old sister. She was pretty and vivacious and had just started going to discos, although she had to be home by eleven.

10

'Julie? I'm not wanting a night out with my kid sister!' Bob said sharply, although Alison knew he loved Julie. 'I wanted to be with you!'

She wanted to say something to make it better, less of a disappointment for him, but even while she was seeking for words, the end of the tea-break bell rang.

'I'll have to go!' she said. 'Please try to understand.'

She expected he would be waiting for her when she arrived home, tired, dishevelled, disappointed and anxious at ten minutes to six. But he was not there and she ran straight upstairs to her mother.

'Are you better? Has the doctor come?'

Mrs Craig turned her head on the pillow and sighed.

'I could have died for all McFaddon seems to care. He's getting too old for his job, that's it. No baby takes this long to appear. You'd better go out and ring him again, Alison. My back is paining so dreadfully.'

'Mother, I'm so sorry! Have you taken your pills?'

'Yes, of course!' Mrs Craig all but snapped the words. 'They don't do me any good. I must have something stronger.'

Alison fluffed up the pillows, and with a last anxious glance at her mother hurried down to the telephone in the hall. She dialled the familiar number of the surgery, hearing it ring a few times; then a receptionist answered.

'Can I help you?'

'Is Dr McFaddon there?' Alison asked. 'He was supposed to come and see my mother, Mrs Craig. I rang this morning.'

'I'm afraid he's not here,' the receptionist told her. 'Dr Boyce, Dr McFaddon's new partner is here.'

'Yes, please, I'm very worried,' Alison replied.

The next voice was English and, despite her concern, Alison was surprised into remarking:

'I didn't know Dr McFaddon was getting a partner!'

The new doctor laughed, a pleasant easy laugh. 'I've obviously been kept a dark secret. You are the third person to say that today. Well, I'll come right away and see your mother. Can I have your address?'

Ten minutes later Doctor Michael Boyce was in his little

Morris, driving along the cobbled streets to the suburb where the Craigs lived. He was frowning slightly, not because he was forced to concentrate on the strange Scottish roads, but because Doctor McFaddon had given him a brief but concise outline on Mrs Craig.

'Bit of a hypochondriac, that one!' he'd told Michael. 'Nothing seriously wrong with her. She gets these attacks from time to time – nothing you can do. In my opinion she exaggerates the pain a lot to get extra attention from that young daughter of hers. Still, you can't be altogether sure, but the x-rays don't reveal any problem.'

An hour ago he'd phoned to say he wouldn't be back for the evening surgery and Michael must take it for him. Michael had only just seen the last patient when Alison Craig had phoned. She'd certainly sounded anxious. Maybe Mrs Craig was worse than his senior partner believed.

Alison opened the front door to him even before he'd rung the bell. She must have been watching for him from a window. Her face – a beautiful, interesting face, he decided at first glance – was tired and worried. He smiled reassuringly as he followed her upstairs.

Alison's first impression of the new young doctor was instantly favourable. He looked calm, efficient and reassuring. It was clear from his voice that he was English. He was of medium height and build, with dark hair and dark-brown eyes. His face was longish, ending with a firm, square chin that was oddly at variance with the gentle curve of his mouth. There was no questioning his good looks, although Alison was far too worried to notice them.

His examination of Mrs Craig was expert and thorough. When it was over he told her that he would give Alison a prescription for some pills which would ease the pain. Then he went downstaris, Alison, greatly relieved, behind him. In the hall he turned suddenly and said:

'Here's the prescription, and you can give your mother one every time she feels restless or in pain. It doesn't matter how often you give them – they are quite harmless.'

'They're not a drug, then?' Alison asked, puzzled.

12

'They are sugar, mostly!' Michael Boyce admitted, watching the girl's face.

'Sugar? But how can that relieve the pain?'

'They are what we call placebos,' the man told her gently. 'You see, I can find nothing wrong with your mother and I'm reasonably certain her pain is entirely in her imagination. If I give her pills that she thinks will cure her pain, so they will, if she wants to be free of it, I mean.'

'I don't understand,' Alison said a little stiffly.

'Your mother believes she is in pain,' Michael Boyce said quietly. 'But Dr McFaddon and I have failed to find anything at all the matter with her. That does not necessarily mean there is nothing wrong but she cannot locate the actual area of pain. When I said to her, "It hurts here, does it?" she said, "Yes!" although that particular part would be quite unaffected had she really suffered from arthritis. When, again, I asked her to show me the area of pain, she pointed to one place which, when I next asked if it hurt, she replied, "No!" Her reply depended on where *I* thought the pain lay, not where *she* knew it lay. Now do you understand?'

Alison felt a rush of colour flooding her cheeks. She had liked this new doctor at first glance. Now she was furiously angry with him.

'You are suggesting my mother is making it all up?' she said in a cold, tight voice.

'Exactly, although once again I repeat that imaginary pain can cause a patient real suffering. It is usually symptomatic of some mental worry. I would imagine that your mother feels worse when things are going wrong. Has anything happened prior to this attack that could have upset her?'

'Far from it!' Alison cried. 'In fact, on the contrary, she has been far better than usual – so much better that I was going out tonight to a party. She doesn't like being left as a rule and she said herself she felt so much better, there was no reason for me to stay with her.'

'But now you are not going?' Michael Boyce said pointedly.

13

'No, of course not!' Alison hesitated, seeing suddenly where his questions were leading. 'No, you're quite wrong, Dr Boyce, if you think my mother has put on this attack just so I couldn't go out with Bob . . . why, it's a horrid suggestion. I *know* she wouldn't do such a thing. I think you'd better ask Dr McFaddon's opinion about a patient he has treated for years. He believes in Mother's attacks and he's certainly had a good deal more experience of them than you have had.'

Michael's mouth tightened but he controlled himself with an effort. He would never have imagined that the pale, tired girl who greeted him on the doorstep had such a temper. Her green eyes were blazing at him and her cheeks were flushed. She looked even more beautiful than he'd first thought, but this was certainly no time to be admiring his patient's daughter.

'I'm sorry you value my opinion so poorly,' he said. 'Believe me, I wouldn't have taken you into my confidence had I believed you would be offended. I had assumed that you could be told the truth – and could face it. Apparently I was mistaken. I'll ask Dr McFaddon to continue treating your mother next time.'

'Please do!' Alison said, suddenly near to tears. And barely giving him time to leave the house, she hurriedly closed the door behind him. She stood with her back against it, feeling her legs trembling with anger.

I hate that man! she thought violently. He must have a horrid kind of mind to say a thing like that. As if Mother would be so selfish – oh, it's beastly!

Unaccountably, she burst into tears. But she did not cry for long. Within a few minutes her head was up again, and she dashed the tears away from her cheeks.

I hope I never see *him* again! she thought, and only then realized that it was after seven and Bob had not telephoned and obviously did not mean to call.

She hurriedly made tea and took a tray up to her mother's room. Mrs Craig seemed better.

'I thought the new young doctor seemed very nice, even

14

if he is an Englishman,' she said, accepting the plate of toasted scones Alison handed to her.

Alison's mouth tightened.

'I didn't like him at all, Mother. I don't think you would either, if you knew what he'd said downstairs.'

Mrs Craig paused with the scone half-way to her mouth.

'What did he say? What has happened, Alison? I thought you were a long time talking to him. And where are my pills he prescribed?'

'I'm not going for them, Mother. They can't possibly do you any good at all. He told me himself they were just sugar. He's an incompetent, rude, unpleasant young man and I'll be very surprised if Dr McFaddon keeps him on for long. If he does he'll certainly lose a lot of his patients pretty quickly.'

'Alison!' Her mother's voice broke sharply into her tirade against Michael Boyce. 'I demand to know what he said. What do you mean about the pills?'

'He doesn't seem to think you are ill at all. I told him he'd better consult Dr McFaddon before he sees any more of his patients. Seems he isn't fit to make a diagnosis on his own!'

Michael Boyce was at that moment consulting his senior partner.

''Fraid I've rather upset the apple-cart, sir,' he said to the older man. 'I'd no idea the daughter would react like that. She seemed so sensible at first.'

'Yes, but she has a blind spot where that mother of hers is concerned. She loves her mother, has devoted her life to her ever since the father died. I could have told you she'd defend that mother of hers to the last ditch.'

'There *isn't* anything wrong, is there?' Michael said, suddenly doubting his own diagnosis.

Dr McFaddon laughed.

'No, not physically. It's mental. And that's more your line than mine, my boy. One of the reasons I took you on. These psychological cases aren't in my field, y'know. In my young days people didn't go in for psychology. I've read about the present medical outlook on the link between physical illness and mental and I think there's a great deal in it. But I'm too old to get the hang of it. You've had specialized training in the subject, so you can deal with the mental ones.'

'I'm afraid it's unlikely Miss Craig will let me in the house again, after what I said!' Michael Boyce said ruefully. 'There's one patient you'll have to handle yourself. Trouble is, I never realized the girl was a patient, too.'

'Alison? Nothing wrong with her, my boy.'

'Oh, but there is, if you'll excuse me. She suffers from a complex – and in her own way she's nearly as sick in mind as her mother. Don't you see, Doc, that girl isn't normal? She doesn't, apparently, rebel against the sacrifices she has to make to look after her mother. She accepts them – and willingly. She's giving up a date tonight with some young man or other without a second thought. And that's the way it will go on if someone doesn't do something soon. How old is she?'

'Alison? Twenty-one, I think.'

'Well, you tell me, how often does that girl get away from the house – mix with other young people of her own age? When did she last have a holiday? I'll bet she hasn't had one in years. She'll go on like this, driving herself, denying herself until suddenly one day she'll wake up and find she's thirty, not twenty. And the old woman, she won't get better, she'll get worse. The girl won't ever marry. My God, what a waste!'

Dr McFaddon looked at his young partner with raised eyebrows, a twinkle in his eyes.

'Wonder if you'd have felt so passionately about her if she'd been as plain as a pike-staff instead of a very pretty young lady!' he commented.

Michael flushed, then laughed.

'All right, maybe not! The fact that she is beautiful makes it *more* of a waste. It infuriates me to see things like this happening to people. It's bad enough when daughters devote themselves exclusively to invalid parents who really *are* invalids. But to waste a life for someone who only imagines they are ill . . .'

16

'Well, it's your line of country, as I said just now. What do you suggest should be done? Telling her the truth doesn't seem to have done much good.'

'Maybe it has!' Michael Boyce said thoughtfully. 'Maybe it has sown one tiny seed of doubt in her mind. Next time she has to give up something special for her mother because of a sudden and unexpected "attack" she'll remember what I said and she'll think, and wonder. You're not to undermine me, Doc. Next time you go, if she asks you point-blank, will you bear out what I said?'

'Well, I won't be quite as brutal as you,' the older man said, smiling. 'After all, if you're going to put them both to rights we don't want to lose them as patients, do we? How d'you suggest we get the mother well – in mind, I mean?'

'We can't, not until the girl faces the truth,' Michael said, leaning forward to outline his opinion. It's my guess that her mother has a *reason* for feeling ill. She doesn't want your attention, or mine. She wants the girl's. From what you've told me, I suspect it's a kind of substitute for the husband she lost. She knows she'll be all alone if Alison marries. The less chance her daughter has to get out and about, the less chance there is she'll meet anyone, fall in love.'

'Trouble with that theory, my boy, is that she already has a boyfriend – known him for years. Everyone takes it for granted they'll marry one of these days. And old Mrs Craig approves!'

For a moment Michael was stumped. Then he said:

'One of these days, but not now, not in the near future. She'll be ill before that happens, mark my words; too ill for the girl to go ahead with wedding plans. I take it the young man believes she's ill, too?'

'As far as I know. Alison told me he was wonderfully kind and understanding.'

'And willing to wait indefinitely!' Michael finished. 'Then he's a fool! If I had a girl like that I wouldn't wait. I'd rush her off her feet. Make her want me so much she'd have no further need for her mother's complete dependence on her. That's a substitute for what she wants. She wants love and

17

children and a home of her own, only she doesn't know it yet. She's emotionally satisfied by her mother's need for her; it satisfies her maternal instinct to love and care for her mother the way she would a child.'

'Seems you know an awful lot about her in one short meeting,' old Dr McFaddon said with another twinkle.

Michael shared in the joke even though it was against himself.

'Well, I'm going to make it my job to know some more,' he said, smiling. 'Now tell me, Doc, was it a boy or a girl you've just brought into the world?'

For the moment he had forgotten Alison as they discussed the unusual delivery. But Alison had not forgotten him.

Three

A lison felt tired and depressed. The dreadful monotony of life in the factory was getting her down. Usually she did not let it. Deliberately she would allow her mind to wander off into impossible daydreams while her hands moved automatically in all too familiar movements at her machine. These daydreams nearly always centred round romantic and imaginary islands in strange, exotic parts of the world. Sometimes she would be lying on a silvery sandy beach, shaded by giant palm trees, listening to the pounding of the great white rollers. Someone beside her would turn to smile at her. Sometimes this man, who was faceless, would gently kiss her lips before putting his arms around her. It wasn't Bob . . . or at least this dream-companion did not act or behave like Bob, who belonged to everyday and to all that was known and safe and ordinary. It was a Bob transformed, as she imagined he might change in such surroundings, just as she, in her mind, would be changed.

Her white hands moving in front of her were tanned golden in her dreams, tanned by a warm, caressing sun. She was beautiful; felt beautiful and worthy of the adoration that was hers for the asking. Not that she ever asked for it in these dreams. Her thoughts shied away from any passion in this friendship. Their conversation was of romantic love; of wonderful things like music, art, literature: noble, worthwhile talks, so very different from the conversation that flowed around her in reality.

Had he known her thoughts, Michael Boyce, who was really a very good psychologist indeed, would have told her she was afraid of life. Deeply romantic by nature, deeply passionate beneath the unawakened surface, Alison was afraid to let love come to her in case it should fail her. She didn't want love and sex if it must mean what the girls around her made it out to be. She wanted no satisfaction of the senses, no cheap clever talk or furtive love-making. She wanted love as the poets she had studied once wrote about it. Second best would never do, and if she could not have what her inner heart demanded she would do without.

Yet she liked the girls with whom she worked. She knew they were kind, generous, well-meaning; and she in no way considered herself 'better' than they – only different. They, too, recognized her as 'different'. They believed she was cold, shy, indifferent to men, that she lacked something essential in the feminine make-up. They did not realize any more than did Alison that it was there, buried deep but far more profound and intense than in themselves.

Alison's particular friend, Betty, was quieter and less flashy than the others. Perhaps the fact that she could only be described as 'plain' by the other girls made her, too, different. They tried to find her dates but somehow they never amounted to anything. After the first date Betty was not asked out again. She clung to Alison because she knew Alison, like herself, was without anyone to talk about while the others discussed their previous evening's entertainment. They all knew, of course, that Alison had a boyfriend, Bob. But perhaps because she went out with him so seldom they did not take this 'steady' very seriously and Alison and Betty were generally treated in the same way by the others, with compassion for the dull lives they led; in Betty's case it was tempered with pity because it was so obvious she did not attract the opposite sex; in Alison's with surprise because she was attractive yet did not seem to *want* to attract the opposite sex.

Betty admired Alison, saw far more in her than did the others. She realized Alison had a far better brain and that really she was wasted in the factory. But she knew about Alison's mother and how necessary the money was, and there was no doubt about the fact that the factory paid well.

She herself would have been incapable of doing any other kind of work, unless she had wanted to be a sales-girl. But her very shyness had prevented her from working in a shop, having to speak to and deal with customers; and so she had come to the factory and found her niche. But she knew Alison did not 'fit'. Romantically, she, too, daydreamed, but the centre of her imagination was her friend. One day some terribly rich and handsome man – a prince, maybe – would fall in love with Alison, sweep her off to his castle in Europe, and Alison would take Betty as a kind of maid, companion. Then she, too, would participate in the glamours of life in a palace or on a yacht or in America; always there at Alison's side.

Strangely enough, it was Betty who was instrumental in bringing Michael Boyce into Alison's life a second time within two weeks. It was shortly before the end of the afternoon shift that the accident happened. Always inclined to be clumsy if she felt she was being watched, Betty's hand slipped as the foreman was making his last round and had paused a moment to watch her. A moment later her fingers were caught in the machine and with one agonized cry the girl fainted and slid to the floor.

It happened so quickly that Alison was hardly aware at first what had occurred. The foreman darted forward and stopped the machine, and as Alison bent to see what was wrong he had already returned with the first-aid kit and was swiftly applying a tourniquet to Betty's hand. Momentarily sickened by the sight, Alison saw that two of Betty's fingers were hanging loose.

But she kept her head, helped the foreman and then, when the bleeding had been arrested, helped him to carry the now semi-conscious girl to the Sick Bay. Betty was obviously in considerable pain as she regained full consciousness and feeling began to return to her damaged hand. The foreman had gone to phone for the doctor and the Sick Bay attendant had given Betty a bromide to subdue the shock.

'Stay with me!' Betty begged Alison, and receiving a nod

of agreement from the nurse Alison sat with her arm around the girl, wishing she could do something to relieve the pain, take some of it into herself.

It seemed hours while they sat there, Betty moaning softly, Alison whispering comforting words, waiting for the doctor. When Michael Boyce walked into the room Alison was momentarily shaken but was still too concerned about her friend to give him more than a passing thought.

The doctor, too, was surprised to find Alison in the Sick Bay. For one moment he was afraid it was she who had had the accident and all but severed two fingers and he felt almost mean when he realized with relief it was the other girl, lying with her head on Alison's shoulder. Then he forgot both girls while he concentrated on giving Betty morphine to put her out of her pain. As soon as she was unconscious he turned to Alison and said:

'She'll have to go to hospital, of course. I'll run her there in my car; it will be quicker than calling an ambulance. Can you come with her?'

'Of course!' Alison said, and then, with a touch of defiance: 'Have I time to scribble a note to my mother? She'll wonder where I am if I'm not home at the usual time. I could get one of the other girls to drop it in on their way home.'

'Two minutes, then,' Michael said, wondering, as he spoke, how deliberately she had brought her mother into the conversation. It was almost as if she had flung down a challenge, and yet that wasn't really fair. She hadn't hesitated to say she would go with her friend.

Five minutes later he was driving the two girls to the large General Hospital. Normally he would have called an ambulance, but he knew how busy they invariably were and they might have had to wait a quarter of an hour or more before one came. He wanted Betty on the operating table before she came round from the morphia injection he had given her.

'Poor kid,' he said aloud. 'I'm afraid she will lose those fingers, and it's her right hand, too.'

'Won't she . . . be able to work in the factory again?'

22

Alison asked from the back seat, where she sat nursing Betty's still form.

'Doubt it. Be some time before she learns to use the other fingers as substitutes and then she'll always be a bit clumsy. Still, she'll get compensation, I expect. How did it happen?'

'I don't quite know. Her hand slipped, I think. I wasn't watching. The machines are quite safe, so long as you pay attention to what you are doing.'

Alison felt annoyed with herself. She had resolved, somewhat childishly, never to speak to this man again, yet here she was, in the back of his car, talking to him quite casually.

'Seems a strange job for you,' he was saying. 'Doesn't the monotony get you down?'

'Sometimes! I stay there because I'm well paid.' Her voice was sharper.

'Yes, I see. But what would you have done if you were not the family breadwinner?'

'I really don't know!' Alison replied coldly and untruthfully. She had no intention of letting this man pry into her private life.

'I don't really believe that!' the young doctor said calmly. 'It doesn't fit you as a person. I cannot imagine you as a young girl, dreaming of the future and seeing a factory as your ultimate aim.'

Alison bit her lip. Somehow this man had the knack of antagonizing her.

'I don't see how it can interest you!' she replied in a tight, cold little voice.

'All the same, it does!' Michael retorted. 'You see, I'm one of those people who hate to see waste.'

'So I'm wasting my life?' Alison rose swiftly to the bait. 'You're not very polite, are you, Dr Boyce?'

'I can be!' Michael said. 'Mostly, in my profession I have to be. But as you pointed out yourself last time we met, you are not my patient, or likely to be, so I don't have to watch my step with you, do I?'

'So you are only polite when it serves your own purpose?' Alison retorted with sarcasm.

23

'Or impolite when it serves my purpose. Now, at least, I have made you talk to me. How is your mother?'

Alison flushed a deep red. She was glad Michael's back was towards her and that he could not see the blush. She could willingly have hit him.

'She's quite well, thank you, despite your last visit.'

'Then perhaps you could come to the cinema with me tomorrow evening?'

Surprise momentarily robbed Alison of words. When she spoke, her voice was not quite so level in its tone.

'I'm sorry. I have another engagement.'

'Oh, the regular. Surely he's used to being let down at the last minute. Couldn't you break the date and come out with me?'

'Really, you're quite incorrigible!' Alison felt the words come out before they could be prevented. 'I've certainly no intention of breaking my date with Bob, and even if I had no date I shouldn't want to come out with you.'

'Would he mind?' Michael asked. 'Is he the jealous type?'

'I don't see—'

'That it's any business of mine!' Michael finished for her. 'But, you see, it is my business. I know very few people up here and certainly no girls to take out on my day off. You are pretty, presentable and unattached. Naturally, therefore, I am interested.'

'Well, you might as well save your interest for someone else!' Alison cried, furious now because she was sure he was teasing her, goading her. She had never disliked anyone more. If it had not been for Betty she would have made him stop the car and let her find her own way home.

'But I don't intend to do so. Why should I?'

'Because . . . because I'm not "unattached",' Alison said. 'As a matter of fact, Bob and I are getting engaged. Now perhaps you'll have the courtesy to leave me alone.'

It was Michael's turn to be surprised. He'd had no idea – and how could he? – that Alison was really in love with this man. He did not like the idea one little bit. Quite suddenly, driving through the busy streets, Alison and the injured girl

24

in the seat behind him, he realized what had happened to him. He'd fallen in love. He was in love with a girl who hated the sight of him and who was just about to become engaged to someone else. The thought frightened and sobered him, and for a moment he said nothing. Could it happen? Could she really be going to marry this other fellow? Was she really in love? Somehow he couldn't, wouldn't believe it.

'You can't!' he spoke his thoughts aloud. 'You just can't.'

In fact, Alison had had no intention of getting engaged to Bob. She'd only said so in order to put this man out of her life for good and all. Now, suddenly, she found herself, as always with this infuriating companion, on the defensive.

'Can't? I don't quite understand. If you mean get engaged to Bob, then there is absolutely nothing whatever to prevent me. Mother approves and it is what Bob and I want.'

And why not? she thought rebelliously. I've a right to get engaged if I wish. Mother can't object. She likes Bob, and we can't go on as we have been doing all these years. I want to get married, have children. But with Bob? Yes, with Bob. I'm sure I love him. There's never been anyone else.

'Don't!' Michael said suddenly and quite distinctly as he turned into the drive of the hospital. 'Don't do it, Alison.'

Before she could reply he had pulled up at the A & E and people were all around them.

'Wait here, I'll take you home!' Michael shot at her, as he jumped out of the car and hurried into the hospital.

But she couldn't, wouldn't, wait. As soon as Betty was safely away on the stretcher she all but ran back down the drive, afraid that any moment he would come out of the hospital and call her, perhaps follow her in the car. She wanted to get away, be alone, have time to think.

She saw a taxi on the road and with rare extravagance hailed it. It would cost quite a bit to get home, but at least she would be safe.

Safe from what? Why should this man have the power to upset her this way? He had no right. She was none of his business. He was rude, impertinent and thoroughly provoking.

Too good-looking, Alison thought unkindly. No doubt he has been able to get away with murder because he's handsome. There was no denying his good looks and one had to be fair about people, even if you did dislike them. Probably he thought he only had to look at a girl to attract her and that's why he treated her the way he did, thinking she'd fall for his charms. Well, he had had his last chance with her. Tonight, if Bob called round, she'd tell him she was willing to get engaged. He'd be happy . . . he loved her just the way she loved him. And what gave Michael Boyce the right to say 'Don't'? He'd never even met Bob, or else he'd know what a good husband he'd make one day.

Furiously, thought raced after thought as she tried to fathom the reason behind that remark; in fact the whole conversation in the car going to the hospital was bigarre. Had he been trying to hit back at her because she'd told him he was no good as a doctor? Did it amuse him to make her angry? If so, he'd certainly succeeded in what he'd set out to do. She'd never felt so angry with anyone in her whole life.

I hate him! she thought. It was the one feeling she could feel sure about. I hated him when he first said those horrible things about Mother, and I hate him even more now I know him better. 'Don't' indeed. I hope he sees my engagement announcement in the local paper. Then he'll see I meant what I said. I'll have it put in in big black type so he can't miss it.

'We're there, miss! This is where you wanted, isn't it?'

Alison saw with surprise that they were outside her own front door. Hurriedly, she paid the driver and went in to her mother. Still keyed up with some strange inner anger, she hurried upstairs and into her mother's room.

'Mother, I'm getting engaged!' she announced in a firm, steady voice. 'My mind is quite made up!'

Four

Mrs Craig looked at her daughter's flushed cheeks and saw the dangerous sparkle in her eyes. What on earth could have happened to Alison? Suddenly afraid, she remembered that the girl from the factory had told her Alison was away to the hospital with Betty and the new young doctor.

'Alison, not – not to Dr Boyce?' she all but whispered the words.

'Dr Boyce?' Suddenly Alison started to laugh, then, as suddenly, to cry. Mrs Craig watched her thoroughly alarmed.

'For goodness' sake, child, pull yourself together. What's the matter with you?'

'I'm sorry,' Alison said, fighting for control. 'I expect it's just shock . . . seeing Betty, and then that horrible man . . . and then you thinking . . .'

'Alison, sit down at once and tell me what this is all about. I demand to know.'

Calmer now, Alison sat down and in a shaky voice, said:

'Unless Bob has changed his mind about wanting to marry me, I'm going to get engaged to him, Mother.'

'Bob! Well, that's a relief!' Mrs Craig said with truth. For one awful moment, she had believed Alison had fallen head over heels in love with the new young doctor. It wasn't impossible for such a thing to happen; he was very handsome and romantic-looking. And Alison was of an age to want romance. Yes, it could have happened.

She herself had once fallen in love, just the same way, with a man she'd only just met. She'd been in a train with her mother, travelling to England. Quite by accident she dropped her gloves as they were sitting down. The man opposite had bent to pick them up for her and when she had looked up into his eyes – eyes just like Alison's – she'd fallen head over heels in love. It had been the same for Alison's father. Somehow during that long journey from Glasgow to London they had managed to find mutual friends, gain her mother's approval to a furthering of their acquaintance when they all returned to Scotland. Three months later they had married and she'd never looked at anyone else, before or since. Love at first sight. It had happened to her. It could have happened to Alison – and if it had – well, she was under no illusions as to the kind of son-in-law Michael Boyce would have made. She'd lose Alison completely and for ever. Whereas Bob – he was weak, weak enough to do whatever Alison wanted. Alison was a good girl; she'd never leave her mother alone.

'Of course, you wouldn't be wanting to get married right away, would you, dear?' she asked tentatively.

Alison shook her head. No, she only wanted to be engaged. She wasn't ready to marry Bob; not yet, anyway.

'I'll go down and get some tea,' she said. 'Maybe Bob will drop by. He said he might.'

She had barely finished washing the dishes when there was a knock on the back door. Guessing it to be Bob, Alison felt suddenly shy and confused. There could be no backing out now and she didn't really want to, but nevertheless she felt ill at ease as Bob came in and, stooping, kissed her gently on the lips.

'Bob!' She leant her cheek against his jacket so that he could not see her eyes. 'Bob, do you really love me?'

Bob's boyish face stared down at the burnished head in surprise.

'You know I do, Alison! What a funny question.'

'Yes, but . . . well, do you really want to marry me, Bob?'

This kind of conversation was so unusual coming from Alison that he was not quite sure how to deal with her. His arms tightened round her and his heart leapt at the thought that now, at long last, maybe she was beginning to feel the same need for him as he had for her.

28

'We'd be married tomorrow if I have my way,' he replied steadily.

Alison gave a shaky little laugh and drew away from him.

'Well, I didn't mean that exactly, but . . . but we could get engaged, Bob.'

He tried not to sound disappointed. After all, although there was no formal engagement, everyone knew already that one day they were going to get married. A formal engagement wasn't much of a step forward, but at least it was something. Maybe Alison would change once their relationship was recognized by their friends – and by her mother. There was Mrs Craig . . .

'What about your mother, Alison?'

'She's quite happy about it, Bob. I spoke to her before tea. She likes you.'

Bob felt complimented. He'd been a little afraid of Alison's mother and not without reason. Everyone spoke of her as a very difficult woman who dominated Alison. He'd always known that he wouldn't have what one might call an easy mother-in-law.

'Shall we go up and tell her – that it's fixed, I mean?' Alison was asking.

'Kiss me first!' Bob demanded, drawing her back into his arms. His mouth came down on hers, gently at first but then more demanding. Alison tried to respond, but somehow she could not feel the same urgent desire that she knew lay behind Bob's kiss. She loved him – yet she just could not let her emotions have free rein. They were engaged, going to be married, with all that entailed. Surely now she should feel something deeper, more urgent and vital than a mere fondness for the man she was engaged to?

Bob let his arms fall to his sides. Alison was strange, not like other girls. Everything about her made a fellow think of and long for some kind of physical response. She looked as if God had made her for man's delight – yet she was always so cool, so controlled. Yes, that was it – completely in control of her emotions. Could it be that beneath the surface she was frigid, indifferent to sex? He didn't want to believe it. He couldn't believe it.

'I've had a horrible day,' Alison said, almost as if she were excusing her reaction to his kiss. 'One of the girls at work was badly hurt. I had to go with her to the hospital.'

That's probably what's wrong, Bob comforted himself as he followed her upstairs. She's overwrought and tired.

He stayed an hour and then, since Alison looked so worn out, he said good night to Mrs Craig and told Alison he'd be going.

'I'll come and see you off,' Alison told him. She felt a strange need to make amends. He'd been so nice, especially to her mother. Dear, dear Bob. She'd make him happy. She really did love him.

As he took her into his arms again, she told him so.

'There's never been anyone else, Bob,' she said.

He was comforted by her words as he had been unable to find comfort from her goodnight embrace.

It'll be different once we are married, he thought, just as he had once thought that it would be different once they were engaged.

The letter was in Alison's pocket all through the morning shift. It was still unopened. She'd over-slept and had had to rush off to work. Later, there had been too many people milling round her at the mid-morning teabreak asking after Betty. Now it was lunchtime and she could find a few moments' privacy in the rest room while the girls were in the canteen.

She knew who the letter was from. Only a doctor could have such appallingly untidy writing. Her cheeks burned at the thought of what the envelope might contain . . . more insulting remarks about her private life, she supposed. Why couldn't he leave her alone, let her live her life in peace without his interference?

She was completely and totally unprepared for the words that danced beneath her eyes.

'*Dearest Alison!*'

She nearly put the letter down, believing it could not be for her after all.

I know you must think me mad, but please, please don't do it. Don't marry a man you can't possibly love, or if you do love him, then still don't marry him because he cannot possibly love you as much as I do.

If you haven't torn the letter up by now, maybe I've still a slight chance to make you understand how I feel. If I've been rude to you, it is only because I had to make you feel something for me, if only anger. I've never been in love before. That's why at first I was angry with you. But I knew it yesterday when you sat in the back of my car with that poor girl – she's going to be all right, by the way!

I know there isn't a reason in the world why you should fall in love with me. But at least give me one chance to show you how nice I can be when I try! Please, Alison, please, before you commit yourself to this engagement. One afternoon, one evening, only an hour, if you like. But give me a chance.

If, on reading this, you think, 'how conceited, how stupid, as if I could ever love a man like that' – (Alison's cheeks burned at how nearly right word for word he had gauged her reactions) – *then you have nothing to fear by meeting me. I swear that I will leave you in peace if you'll grant me these few hours. If you do not, then I shall know, you are afraid to trust yourself with me, and I shall keep on pestering you. Blackmail, I know! But all is fair in love and war and you are so fair and I am so much in love.*

Michael

She sat down suddenly, the letter screwed into a ball, her face flushed and perturbed. How could she deal with a man like Michael Boyce? He was utterly unpredictable. Nothing he did or said was like other people's behaviour. She'd only met him twice and now this letter, pouring out his love for her. How could he possibly be in love with someone who was all but a stranger to him? And yet . . . yet it sounded sincere. He must have rushed home from the hospital, scrawled off the letter and rushed out again to catch the evening post. Otherwise it could not have reached her home next morning.

He was mad, unbalanced. And he a doctor, too! He wasn't even very young – thirty at least, yet he wrote like a love-smitten schoolboy. *You are so fair and I am so much in love.* The words repeated themselves in her mind, causing her cheeks to flush once more a deep pink. These weren't the words of a schoolboy . . . *a few hours . . . afraid to trust yourself . . .*

What good could that do? It was absurd, completely absurd to even suggest such a thing. Yet if she refused, he would always believe she couldn't trust herself. And if she went, how would he behave? Would he try to make love to her?

I *am* afraid! Alison thought in sudden alarm. Her whole body was trembling in nervous anticipation. How well he guessed her feelings. Yet he was wrong about one thing . . . Bob. What right had he to say, 'Don't marry a man you can't possibly love!' She'd always loved Bob, always would. Then why be afraid? Why not tell Michael Boyce so, calmly and sensibly, and then he would leave her alone? He'd promised. Then she could forget about him, put him out of her mind completely.

She felt calmer. Yes, she would go. Hitherto their conversations had been sparring matches, two people each trying to make the other angry. This time she would be completely unemotional. He would see that she knew her own mind and heart. Obviously he was a little mad. Perhaps he had been alone too much. No sane person could imagine himself in love with a girl they'd only met twice, and then in anger! She could point this out to him and he would see how right she was.

Impulsively, she ran down to the canteen and bought a postcard and a pencil.

I'll meet you at the corner of my road at two thirty on Saturday.

Yours sincerely, Alison

She borrowed a stamp and hurriedly posted the card before she could change her mind. Then she went back to the rest room to uncrumple the letter and read its strange contents once again.

A dozen times that day, at least, she regretted that impulsive reply. She thought of writing another card, cancelling the appointment. During the film Bob took her to that evening, she followed nothing of the story as her mind composed a suitable reason for not going after all. Once or twice when Bob spoke to her, she had to force her mind back to what he was saying.

By the time she was in bed she was too exhausted to think coherently. She fell quickly into a deep sleep, only to wake to the problem again next day.

I'm being absurd and childish! she told herself as she hurriedly made her mother's breakfast and took up the tray. I said I would go, and I will!

Mrs Craig took the tray from her daughter's hands and said depressingly:

'I had such a bad night, Alison; couldn't sleep at all. Do you think you could call in at Dr McFaddon's surgery on your way home and pick me up some more of my tablets?'

A denial rose swiftly to Alison's lips but died there, unspoken. What reason could she give her mother for avoiding the surgery at all costs?

'Haven't you any left?' she asked hesitantly.

Mrs Craig looked at her sharply.

'Of course not, dear. I told you I had run out last evening. I don't know what's the matter with you lately; all of a dither and no memory at all. I suppose that's what love does to a girl.'

Love! Alison's cheeks flushed a deep pink and then faded quickly as she realized her mother was alluding to her engagement to Bob.

'Now write it down, Alison, or tie a knot in your handkerchief – "I must call at Dr McFaddon surgery for Mother's tablets".'

'Yes, I won't forget!'

Hurriedly, she bade her mother goodbye and ran downstairs. Would Michael be there? Would she run into him by accident? She hoped not. Tomorrow, Saturday, would be quite soon enough.

But it couldn't come quickly enough for Michael Boyce. He'd staked everything on this meeting with Alison. Somehow he had to find some way to persuade her not to go through with this engagement to her childhood sweetheart. She mustn't! Deep within him, he *knew* Alison was meant for him, Dr Michael Boyce. But how to persuade her to know it, too. He'd made such an appalling mess of things at the start. If only he'd known more about her at that first meeting; known then that he was going to fall in love with her, he'd never have antagonized her about her mother. Now he was beginning with a hefty handicap. Not only did Alison dislike him, but she didn't trust him, either.

He clung to the hope that she must feel something, otherwise why agree to meet him? Had it been only to prove to him that she was no coward? That she had faith in her love for Bob and his for her?

He tried to put her from his mind as he coped with the usual rush of Friday evening's surgery. Already the waiting-room was full and he was single-handed. Dr McFaddon was once again out with a patient. He'd only the nurse, Diane Fellows, to help him.

Diane Fellows was a young widow. Her husband had been one of Dr McFaddon's patients and it had been a pretty sad case, Fellows dying at the early age of thirty-eight of leukemia. His young wife had been a nurse before her marriage and, providentially, had taken up her career again soon after her husband's death. She was an attractive young woman – a year or two older than Michael – cool, sophisticated and efficient. His senior partner had enlightened him as to Diane's background before he met her and prepared him not to ask questions about her husband.

'Adored him! Nursed him devotedly until the end came. She'll never get over it, made me promise not to mention his name.'

He'd not paid much attention to her after this, treating her with the same quiet professional manner as she treated him. He felt vaguely sorry for her but tried not to show it. She was so obviously trying hard to hide her inner grief. Successfully, too, for she was always composed and even-tempered, even on busy nights like this, when patients could be pretty trying.

'Over thirty, I'm afraid!' she told him as he sat down behind his desk, a faint apologetic smile on her face. 'But at least ten of them are for prescriptions. Shall we get rid of them first?'

Michael nodded. This was the usual routine. He sat signing forms, barely noticing the patients who stood waiting while Diane handed their cards to him, until suddenly a name on the form jumped up at him as if written in large black letters. Mrs Craig, 3 The Avenue, Carey Street. Alison's mother.

He looked up and saw Alison standing there, silently. His heart gave a lurch.

'Hello!' he said, awkwardly. 'Nothing wrong with you, I hope?'

'Miss Craig is here for her mother's sleeping-pills,' Diane's cool voice interjected smoothly.

'Yes, yes, of course. Won't keep you a moment. By the way, thanks for the card.'

Alison flushed, a schoolgirl trait which gave her inner feelings away, both to the young doctor and to the nurse. She could think of no suitable reply, but stood waiting until Michael handed her the required prescription. Then with a barely audible goodnight, she went quickly out of the room.

'You seem to have scared the life out of her,' Diane said with a half-smile. 'She's usually quite chatty with Dr McFaddon.'

Michael looked up at the nurse, and away again quickly. There was something . . . well, almost spiteful in the last remark; and it wasn't like Diane to make personal remarks. Nevertheless, he was glad to be able to speak of Alison.

'You've known Miss Craig long?' he asked.

Diane shook her head, a wisp of dark hair falling from

beneath her nurse's cap on to the smooth white skin of her forehead.

'No, only by sight. She's younger than I am. I'm thirty, you know.'

Michael hadn't known and found it difficult to believe. The girl looked very little older than Alison, yet at the same time there was something in her face which made her seem far more mature. Was it the serenity of those slightly eastern slanting eyes? Or in the curve of her mouth?

Aware that he had been staring, he turned eyes away, faintly surprised that Diane had held his glance so long without looking away herself. Strange girl. He sighed. Maybe all women were strange in their separate ways and incomprehensible to man! To him anyway.

'Well, this won't do!' he said with a sudden sigh. 'Better have the next one in, Nurse.'

Diane Fellows turned away, strangely disappointed. What had she been hoping for? she asked herself as she moved towards the waiting-room door. Some personal remark? Anything, anything at all to show that he had noticed her. He'd been here two months and to all intents and purposes she might as well be a piece of the surgery equipment.

Suddenly, she hated the uniform she wore; hated the very name 'Nurse'. It hid from the world her femininity, made her just a unit in the cog of a medical wheel. She'd felt that way before she'd married Peter. One of the reasons she had married him was to do away with that uniform for ever, to become a woman, a real woman . . . and what a fiasco that had all turned out to be. Even their honeymoon had been an unutterable failure. Peter, the man who spoke such wonderful words of love, had been quite unable to express himself physically. As if words were enough for her! Within a year, she knew she'd married a sick man, a dying man. Maybe it had been her punishment for marrying a man she'd never really loved. And yet, if Peter had been a real man, able to satisfy her, how differently it might have worked out. As it was, she felt cheated, done out of the best years of her life. As Peter lay dying, his words of love could no longer move

36

her. Coolly and efficiently, she nursed him, ministering to his every need except that one vital need he had of her love.

'You don't care, Diane, you don't really care at all.' How often had he spoken those words; how often had she parried them with:

'Don't excite yourself, Peter. You know it's bad for you.'

But he knew. As his body died, so his mind seemed to become especially alive until he seemed able to see through her.

'I ought not to love you. There's little about you to love, yet, God help me, I do. You're hard, Diane, hard and cruel. You have a beautiful body but no mind. You're like a gorgeous animal. I'm glad now we never had any children. I think they might have been the kind to tear off butterflies' wings or cut up worms, just for the sadistic pleasure of watching them squirm. I shan't be sorry to die.'

Well, she had done her duty, and now, thank heaven, she was free again; free to find some other man; someone far better suited than poor intellectual Peter to be her mate. Michael Boyce was the incarnation of her hitherto unfulfilled dreams. She'd wanted him from the first moment when Dr McFaddon had introduced him and he'd held her hand in that strong, firm grasp. It had tortured her day and night. 'Nurse this' and 'Nurse that', he said, never, as did so many of the young doctors in hospital before she was married: 'Come on, Nurse, what's your real name? Doing anything after duty tonight, Nurse?'

She knew she attracted men . . . all men. She knew that they nearly knew she would give them what they wanted.

'There's something primitive about you, Diane, Peter had once said. You seem to promise so much. You're so completely feminine!'

He'd been wrong, of course. She hadn't a woman's gentleness, tenderness, maternal instincts. She would have left Peter if it hadn't been for his illness and then it hadn't been pity that had kept her nursing at his bedside. She'd been penniless, the daughter of a retired postman, when she married Peter. He came from a well-off family, and although he hadn't

37

much money of his own to leave her Diane had guessed correctly that his relations would never let his widow starve. After his death they'd guaranteed her a nice little income for life, or until she married again.

'You've been so wonderful, so devoted!' Peter's mother had said. 'We all feel this is the least we can do. Of course, we know you won't be able to bear the thought of marrying again, not just now, but later on, dear, you may wish to do so. We wouldn't blame you. You are young and very pretty and Peter would not have wanted you to go on grieving for him.'

As if she had grieved! She'd been so thankful she could have cried from relief. But money wasn't everything. She'd give it up without a qualm – if the right man came alone. And now he had. Granted Michael wasn't earning much yet, but she knew he would. He was no dreamer like Peter. He was strong and forceful and ambitious. He'd go far and she intended to go with him. There must be a way – some way to make him notice her. She'd find that way, sooner or later. Meanwhile there was a job to do and efficiently. She didn't want to lose those few hours in Michael's company. In a way his very indifference to her added spice to the challenge she had to take up; and win.

Somehow, the patients began to thin out and soon it was the last one.

'That's the lot!' Michael said, leaning back in his chair. 'Gosh, I could do with a drink!'

'I've made some coffee,' Diane said. 'Or if you think you can walk a couple of hundred yards I could give you that drink in my flat.'

Michael looked up, startled. He was so surprised he could not think what his answer would be. What could have prompted her invitation? Had she meant it? Was she perhaps lonely, wanting company to stave off those tragic memories? Or was it just an impulse?

'Really!' she said quietly, a half-smile on her lips. 'I'd be glad if you'd accept. I could do with a drink, too.'

He noticed her now as a woman. Diane knew the difference

38

in the sideways glance. She held his gaze, her eyes enigmatic, very faintly smiling.

'Nurses can drink, off duty,' she said smiling.

Michael smiled, too.

'Don't I know it! Like troopers at the hospital I was at. Right, I'd enjoy a drink; I'm exhausted.'

'I'll get my things,' Diane said, no trace in her voice of her inner elation. 'I won't be a moment.'

Michael was further surprised by her flat. Quite unlike the usual 'digs', it was smart, comfortable and quite luxuriously equipped. Diane pointed to a cocktail cabinet at the side of the room and indicated a variety of bottles.

'Perhaps you'll mix up something while I get out of this uniform,' she said, disappearing into another room and allowing him time to look around him.

Her reappearance was a further surprise. In fact, for a moment, he thought some friend must share the flat with her. In place of his 'nurse' was an incredibly beautiful woman. The dark hair that had occasionally shown beneath the nurse's cap was now flowing round her shoulders in an unfashionable but quite startling cloud. It accentuated the amazing whiteness of her skin. She was wearing a low-cut evening sweater with tight leopard-skin slacks. Each fantastic curve of her body was deliberately outlined. Michael never realized quite how deliberate was her intent to make this impact.

'You're – stunning, Diane!' he said, leaning forward and handing her a drink. 'Here's to Beauty.'

'And here's to the Beast,' Diane replied, curling up in the chair opposite him and smiling at him through a dark wave of hair falling across one smooth, ivory cheek.

'Well, let's hope not that!' Michael grinned back. 'Surely that's not your opinion of all men? Only of doctors, I trust.'

'Well, medical students!' Diane said, sipping her drink. 'My opinion of men during my hospital days was not of the highest order.'

'Nor mine of nurses,' Michael chipped back. 'Though I can't say I'd blame the medical students in your case, Diane.'

'Thank you! I shall take that as a compliment. Oh, this is nice. I needed that drink. Let's have another.'

'Well, one more, than I must push off. My landlady isn't too pleased when I'm late for supper.'

'You don't want to let landladies bully you,' Diane said, pouring two more drinks and brushing past Michael as she gave him his glass. 'Women respect a man who wears the pants and landladies are women, you know.'

Michael laughed again, feeling relaxed and stimulated. He'd had no idea Diane could be like this. Life had been pretty dull, dreary and colourless since his arrival in Scotland. Here was suddenly a little oasis of sophistication. Besides, it helped him not to think too much about tomorrow – about Alison.

'I'm not so sure you're right, Diane,' he answered her last remark. 'Last time I spoke my mind to a girl I really got the brush off. Do you honestly believe women enjoy being bullied?'

'Some – probably most! A girl likes to be able to respect a man, feel he's the master. Primitive, I suppose. But that's part of the fun; the giving, the surrender, the allowing of complete physical domination.'

'But not mental domination?' Michael parried, laughing.

'That's different. After all, a woman has a mind of her own and ought to use it.'

'Equality when it suits them,' Michael said. 'But I don't think these facts relate to landladies. I really ought to go.'

'Why not stay here and eat with me? It gets so lonely eating on your own night after night.'

She looked suddenly very young, helpless and lonely, and he was reminded swiftly of her widowhood. Poor kid! Of course it must be hard for her. Hard in lots of ways.

He was on the point of agreeing when Diane, pushing her advantage too far and too quickly, said:

'Please, Michael, *please!*'

There was something personal and urgent in the tone of her voice, in the first-time use of his Christian name, which instantly put their relationship on a different footing. Until

40

then they had been like two friends, easily and quickly acquainted, enjoying a drink together and stimulated by their repartee. Now it had changed. She didn't want just anyone to stay for dinner – she wanted him. He realized for the first time that she was interested in him not just as a friend, but as a man. He couldn't let himself get involved with Diane. He was in love with Alison, and that being so he had nothing to offer Diane, nothing of a lasting nature.

He stood up, looking down at her regretfully.

'I'm awfully sorry,' he said quietly. 'But I really do think I should go. It was sweet of you to invite me and perhaps another time . . .'

She knew her mistake and was furious with herself. Men liked to do the chasing and she'd broken the golden rule. Hiding her chagrin, she stood up, smiling easily and naturally.

'Of course! Any time you feel like a drink, just drop in. As a matter of fact, I'd planned to wash my hair tonight, anyway, so maybe it's best this way.'

Contrarily, Michael regretted his hasty departure as soon as he was on his way home. Why run away like that? Diane obviously knew her way around and there was no real reason why he should not have stayed. Of course, there were the gossips. Someone might have seen him coming out of her flat late, and being a doctor he had his reputation to consider! Better, another time, to invite Diane out to a meal. Perhaps if Alison would agree they could make up a foursome with some other man, drive in to Edinburgh, maybe, and dine and dance. It might be fun.

But would Alison agree? What about that mother of hers?

Suddenly dispirited, Michael let himself into his rather dreary digs and braced himself to meet his landlady.

'Well!' she greeted him. 'About time, too. The cauliflower soup's quite cold.'

41

Five

The afternoon started badly for Alison. First, her mother kept cross-questioning her as to where she was going.

'I have some shopping to do, Mother. I won't be long.'

She couldn't bring herself to tell Mrs Craig where she was going, because her mother so disliked Michael Boyce she would undoubtedly make a scene. All the same, she hated telling a lie.

Then she had difficulty in choosing what to wear. She had so few clothes – there was little money to spend on them – and this afternoon she did particularly want to look mature, sophisticated, sure of herself. If she could only decide between last year's blue jersey dress, which was smart but beginning to look past its best, and this year's grey linen which was new but which somehow had not the cut or style of the blue dress.

Finally, she wore the blue and then found her last pair of nylons. Pulling them on too fast, she snagged one toe. Feverishly, conscious of passing time, she took a last hurried look at her reflection, ran downstairs only slowing her pace as she neared the end of the avenue.

She could now see Michael's car parked by the pillar-box. But also on the opposite side of the road she could see Bob approaching. Of all the bad luck to run into Bob *now*! There was no chance that she could reach the car before Bob saw her, unless of course she ran.

Anxious to avoid a series of awkward questions from Bob, she ran. Hurriedly, breathless, she pulled open the door of Michael's car and said:

'Please drive away, quickly, anywhere. Please.'

42

Michael obediently slipped the car into gear and they moved off, leaving Bob alone and unsure of his eyes. Surely it couldn't have been Alison, getting into some man's car, and yet he could have sworn. . .Puzzled, he went on towards Alison's house.

In the car Alison fought to regain her breath.

'I'm sorry!' she said after a moment. 'I was running.'

'Yes, but why?' Michael asked with genuine curiosity. 'I hardly dare hope it was in anxiety to see me.'

Alison sat upright and glared at the profile next to her.

'Now, if you're going to start—'

'I'm sorry!' Michael broke in. 'It's just that I can't seem to help it with you. Believe me, I don't want to make you angry – anything but! Please tell me why you were running.'

'Because Bob was coming down the road on the opposite side,' Alison said truthfully.

'Bob?'

'Yes, my . . . my fiancé.'

Michael was momentarily silenced. So she really was engaged. Things didn't look too good for him. Yet why should she run away from the fellow? He asked her.

'Because I don't think he would have understood. . . this meeting, I mean!' Alison floundered. 'I hadn't told him and it would have been difficult to explain.' Suddenly, in a flare of anger, she cried: 'After all, it *is* very silly, and quite pointless. I don't know why I did come.'

'Please, don't feel sorry about it! If you knew how much your coming means to me, you'd never have hesitated at all.'

Alison stole a quick glance at the man beside her. She had known this would not be easy, but it was clearly going to be even more embarrassing than she had feared.

'I didn't come because you wanted me to,' she said, trying to be truthful. 'It was really only to tell you that there isn't any point in our seeing each other again. You . . . you said I was afraid to tell you so to your face.'

'Go on, then!' Michael challenged her. 'Tell me. Say: I love him and no other man could move me. Tell me that if

43

I were to kiss you, you would feel nothing, nothing at all. Tell me that it doesn't disturb you when I tell you I'm in love with you.'

'Please, please don't.'

Her voice was barely above a whisper. Suddenly determined, Michael swung the car to the left and drove steadily out into the country. Within five minutes, he had the car parked in a farm track and the engine switched off. He turned in his seat and stared down at the girl's white face.

'Go on, Alison. I'm waiting.'

But he didn't wait. Before she could speak, he bent his head and kissed her, not gently but fully and passionately, as he had so much longed to do ever since he'd known himself in love with her.

For one long moment Alison fought against him, trying with her small frantic hands to push him away. But gradually her whole body began to tremble and she felt that she must surely faint soon. One half of her mind still resisted him, yet at the same time she felt her arms go round his neck, pulling him even closer against her and then, at last, returning his kiss.

Suddenly Michael drew away from her and gripped the steering-wheel with both hands so that the knuckles showed taut and white.

'I love you so much, it hurts to kiss you,' he said quietly.

Alison clenched her two hands together in her lap, trying to still their trembling and the trembling of her legs. She felt hopelessly confused by what had just happened. It was so different from what she had expected, planned.

'You shouldn't. . . you shouldn't—' She broke off, unable to voice her emotions.

'Don't!' Michael broke in roughly. 'I know you don't love me, but I'll swear you don't love that Bob of yours either. I had to kiss you, Alison. I hoped to make you wake up to the truth, to yourself, to life, to me. All right, so I've failed to behave as you think I should, but at least you did feel something. I'm sorry, I'll take you home.'

He felt wretched, filled with a hopeless kind of despair.

It was true he had evoked a physical response in this girl but that wasn't what he had wanted! He wanted her love, and her heart was as cold towards him as her body had been warm and alight. How bitter-sweet that kiss had been! And now she was hating him for it.

Alison was so confused she could not think. A moment ago he had been the only reality on earth. Even now, she felt she must hold her arms tightly against her sides to prevent them reaching out to him, demanding another kiss, a renewal of that incredible magic that had flowed through her whole body.

She had never felt this way with Bob. Perhaps it meant that she had never loved him? She did not know how to cope with these strange emotions, of which she'd never been aware before. Was it right or wrong to feel this way? Already the man beside her had apologized. He was sorry, and she, too, should be. He'd believed that such a sudden assault on her might make her realize she loved him, Michael Boyce, and not Bob. Yet all he had succeeded in doing was to make her doubt her love for the man to whom she was engaged.

Suddenly helpless, she turned towards him with a little cry.

'What *is* love? How can one be sure? Oh, I don't understand!' She sounded so young, so bewildered, it caught at Michael's heart in a great overwhelming tenderness for her.

Gently, he reached out and took both her hands.

'If you loved, you would know, Alison. I cannot put it into words for you. It is so many things, a delight, a torment, a longing, an anguish; a pain, a beauty, a feeling that at last life has meaning, purpose. One wants to give and give and give to the loved one and that means desire, too, since to give fully must be to give the body as well as the heart and mind. I've only known these feelings since you came into my life. Even now, I know that nothing can ever be the same again for me. Don't ask me how I know, Alison, but I do know I love you – the way a man is supposed to love a woman. I want you for my wife, to love, to cherish, to care for . . . yes, and to possess. I want my children to be yours,

45

Alison. I want to stride ahead and be a success for you. You fill me with ambition and hope and desire and complete despair, for I know you could never love me. Why should you?'

Something deep within Alison's heart stirred at his words. Never in the years they had known each other had Bob spoken to her like that. He was shy, awkward, inarticulate and his protestations of love were matter of fact and had had no power to disturb her. It was Michael's sudden humility which touched in her heart a new core of feeling, roused in her a tenderness, an excitement, a response that was as new to her as the desire she had felt just now in his arms. It was strange and not a little frightening what powers this man had to evoke in her immediate response; anger, desire, dislike, and now . . . could it be love?

He watched the play of emotions on her pale face as these thoughts chased across her mind. Uncertainly, he tried to guess their truth. What did she feel for him? Certainly not indifference. Was there hope for him after all?

'Alison!'

She turned to face him, startled by the sudden roughness of his voice.

'Alison, marry me. I know that will sound crazy to you, but deep down inside I know we belong together; I *know* it. Let me take care of you. I know you don't feel the same way about me but I think you might, could, if you would only let yourself. I love you so very much.'

'I can't . . . I couldn't . . . I'm engaged to Bob . . . it's madness!' The words of protest tumbled out one after another as if doing so they might protect her from some inner fear. She was suddenly terribly afraid of love. No longer did it seem the easy pleasant undermanding emotion she had experienced in Bob's company. Now love stood for a strange violence, pain, as Michael had said, and an ecstasy which she had never realized before and now only half understood.

'Engagements can be broken! Alison, don't turn your head away from me. Look at me! Let me see in your eyes if you love me at all.'

'I don't . . . I hate you!' Alison burst out desperately. 'I disliked you from our first meeting.'

'Only because I present a challenge. I offer you not the calm security of the known, but the excitement of the unknown,' Michael retorted quickly. 'You are afraid, not just of me, but of life, of love. Don't let fear of becoming a full and complete person hold you back from life. You'll be so sorry in the long, long years ahead. Old people, Alison, seldom regret the experiences of life they undertook, even if they were wrong ones. They regret the experiences they have missed and there's no going back. Because you are so young, you haven't thought of the future. Only half alive, how many all the years ahead seem. Yet those same years spent in happy companionship and love – they aren't long enough.'

All too clearly Alison heard his words and her mind could no longer escape the image of a future married to Bob; long winter nights sitting opposite him, watching television, hearing him talk about his work, thinking of the next day's meals. And children, Bob's children, ordinary quiet family life, sharing a home yet without any deep-down over-whelming love and understanding and need of each other. Was this really what she wanted? Or did that passionate heart, so long subdued, cry out deep within her for all that Michael offered? To love, to feel, to belong, to share, to need, to desire with one's whole being.

'If I could be sure—' she began, but Michael interrupted her with a quick grasp of her hands.

'No one can be completely sure a marriage will be happy! No one can be sure love will last. It isn't a static thing, Alison, it lives and grows and expands, or sometimes it shrinks and slowly dies.'

She looked at him fully then, her hands now holding his as tightly as his held hers.

'Yet you are sure you love me?'

He gave a sudden very sweet smile.

'Yes, I am sure. I've had so much longer than you to think about it, Alison. Until today you've been too busy thinking about how much you hate me.'

47

'I don't hate you now!' The words were out before she had considered them. Hearing them, she knew what she said was true.

'Then go a step further; let yourself fall in love. Alison!'

Her name died on his lips as his mouth came down to hers. Instinctively, her arms went back around his neck and she clung to him tightly, giving him kiss for kiss, no longer caring why she should feel this way. All that mattered was his nearness, his touch.

'Say you love me,' he murmured as he kissed her again and again. 'At least tell me you want me, Alison, darling.'

'I do! I do!' Alison whispered back for there could be no doubting any longer how desperately her body longed to respond more fully to his touch. Now, with complete abandon, she drew his head down once more so that she could feel his lips crushing hers, hurting her with the pain and the pleasure in equal parts.

'Don't – we mustn't. You don't know what kissing you does to me. God, I love you so much! Alison, you must, *must* marry me. I can't live without you; I can't work, sleep. I'm haunted and tormented by thoughts of you day and night.'

Trembling, she sought to control her own violent feelings. Somewhere there must be sanity, calm and collected thought. She knew that but for Michael's wish to protect her, their violent kissing might have led to fuller embraces, perhaps even complete surrender. She sensed his need and knew without doubt that within herself there was the same need. Both were finding it hard to control themselves and Michael's voice, protesting his love for her, only weakened her further.

Was this love? This mad racing of the pulses, this weakness, this trembling need, this desire to give, and to take? Or was it just physical attraction? How could she judge when she had had so little experience of life? How right Michael was! Until today she had not really lived nor felt nor been a woman. By comparison, Bob's goodnight kisses were those of a brother. He had never made her feel this way. And this could be the only way now. To give oneself

48

with indifference – she knew in this moment of truth that it could never happen to her.

'I . . . I'll break my engagement to Bob.' She whispered the words. 'I couldn't go through with it now.'

Michael leant back against the seat of the car, drawing in his breath on a deep sigh of relief.

'I'm so glad, so *glad*,' he said.

'But it doesn't mean I'm in love with *you*!' Alison said swiftly. 'I need time, Michael, time to sort out my feelings. I wouldn't ever marry you, not unless I could be sure that what is between us is love, and not just an attraction.'

'I can wait!' Michael cried, his heart filled now with an immense happiness. 'I *know* there's something more between us than wanting each other. We belong, Alison, I just know it. Oh, darling, I'm going to take you home. I don't think I can stand more happiness now.'

'Mother will be wondering where I am,' Alison said, but, strangely, the thought carried no real conviction. Her mother seemed completely remote from this. But to Michael, Mrs Craig was a sudden reminder of what had first caused trouble between them. He knew that he would have to be immensely tactful with Alison about her mother. No more rash statements, no more fights about her. After all, Mrs Craig could well influence Alison at this crisis in her life, and if Alison gave way this time, there wouldn't be another chance.

'Would your mother let me come and see her? I'd like to apologize,' he said. 'I hope that in future we might even be friends!'

Alison looked at him gratefully.

'Would you? I'm afraid – well, I was so angry with you I told Mother what you'd said that first time you came to see her. Now, naturally, she is biased against you. Michael, you don't really believe she is shamming, do you? You were mistaken in your diagnosis?'

She had asked him the one question he most dreaded from her. His innate professional honesty forbade him lying. So easy to say, 'Yes, I was wrong!' and it would be passed over and forgotten. Yet he couldn't do it. He couldn't lie to her.

49

'In a way!' he prevaricated. 'Look, Alison, I could lie – it would make it easier for me. You must know, now you understand how I feel about you, that I would do anything to avoid antagonizing you now!'

She nodded her head but remained silent.

'Then you will appreciate that what I say must be what I truly believe. I am a doctor, and I can't lie about this, even though I may make you angry. There are lots of people in the world, particularly in this present world where things are so difficult and sometimes hopeless, who sincerely believe they are ill. They want to be ill in their subconscious minds because by doing so, they are counteracting some frustration, acquiring some compensation for something else in life which is wrong. No, let me finish, Alison. These people more often than not don't know they are deliberately cultivating illness. In their imagination they are ill and gradually the subconscious belief impels itself on the conscious mind until they believe, quite genuinely, that it is true.'

'You think this is what Mother does?'

'Yes, I do! But this is the important thing, Alison. They do in fact feel pain. Some people even develop symptoms of the illness they have fabricated. Take, for instance, a woman who desperately wants a child and can't have one. There have been many cases where such a woman has developed all the outward signs of pregnancy, merely from wishful thinking. No one "pretending" pregnancy would want to suffer sickness, for instance, yet these women are sick. They actually feel sick. I believe your mother actually feels pain, but it isn't really there, Alison, only in her mind.'

'Yet Dr McFaddon has treated her for years for arthritis.'

'Yes! Many doctors are forced to do this. They haven't time or, often enough, the psychiatric knowledge, to bring about a real cure, so they treat imaginary ills with imaginary medicines. Just as your mother can believe she feels pain, so she can believe the pills she takes relieve pain. It is a form of self-hypnosis and similar, in reverse, of course, to Christian Science beliefs. They believe that pain does not exist and so convince themselves they are not ill when really they are. People hypnotize themselves into believing they are in love because they need love, a husband, a home, children. I supposed you knew the truth about your mother's illness, or I would never have spoken to you as I did when I called to see her.'

Alison sat perfectly still, her hands now ice cold where a few minutes before they had been warm and alive. Something in Michael's quiet professional voice impressed her with its truth. He was no longer a man but a doctor and one in whom, suddenly, she had faith.

'But why . . . *why* should Mother *want* to be ill? It doesn't make sense!'

'But it does, it always does in these cases,' Michael told her. 'Maybe it began when your father died. She loved him very much, didn't she?'

Alison nodded.

'She had a complete breakdown and I don't doubt the conflict in her mind started them. She wanted to die, too, and yet she couldn't because there was you, only a young girl, to look after. She must, for your sake, go on with the struggle alone. And then slowly but surely your love and care for her when she was so ill with grief, made its impression on her. She need not, after all, struggle alone. She had you to lean on, to love her. But how long would you go on doing so once she was up and about again? Children can be selfish and you were growing up. There would be friends, outside interests to take you away from her.'

Alison shivered.

'You make her out to be so selfish!'

'No, Alison! All this happens deep down inside the mind. After all, what point could there be in the childless woman deliberately affecting symptoms of pregnancy? She would *know* such a thing must be useless in the end.'

'Then Mother only thinks she is ill? She isn't really?'

'Ill in her mind, Alison. She is as much deserving of your sympathy and care as a person really ill – more perhaps. But the longer you give way to her the more reason you give her to be ill next time she wants to keep you beside her. You

51

are very lovely, Alison. She must see that and it threatens her security, for one day some man is going to make you his wife and when you fall in love, how much time will you have for *her*?'

'Yet she agreed to my engagement to Bob!'

'Maybe she understands you better than you do yourself. She knows, or perhaps only senses, that you are not really in love with him. He constitutes less danger to her than someone with whom you were madly and passionately in love.'

'It's...it's horrible!' Alison cried. 'I don't want to believe you.'

'It is human nature, my darling. And it only shows how much your mother needs love and care and understanding.'

'Why do you tell me all this? I'd rather not know.'

'That, too, is human nature!' Michael said, smiling. 'But you asked me to tell you I thought my diagnosis wrong. It doesn't benefit me to tell you the truth; on the contrary, I stand to lose you for the second time. But I'm truthful for your sake as well as for hers. If she is ever to live without fear of losing you, she must learn to stand on her own feet. Can't you see that? She needs interests and companionship that have nothing to do with you. Supposing you were to die, Alison? What would happen to her? As she is now, it would really be the end of her life. That is all wrong. She has excluded everything from her life except you, and when you go there will be nothing.'

'But I shan't go; not while she needs me!' Alison cried.

'But the day might come when you want to go, darling. Suppose you were already married, had children and one of them became ill. Suppose your doctor advised that the child must go to a different climate or it would never get well. What could you do then? Suppose you should decide to marry a doctor, like me, and he were to be offered an important job elsewhere. Are you going to let him go alone while you stay with your mother? No, Alison, *no*. Parents should have some claim on their children's affections and it would be selfish and wrong if they did not receive it, but you have

52

only one life to lead and marriage, a home, children are your due, just as once they were your mother's. The way things are now it is bad for you and bad for her, too. You are helping and encouraging her to lead a completely selfish and useless life. When the end comes what pride or satisfaction can she have? And if you give up the idea of marriage, remain with her and become an old maid, what kind of despair and loneliness will be her legacy to you when she goes?'

'But how could I change now? Even if you are right, it is too late.'

'It isn't – it never is too late, not if your mother can be made to *want* to be well. Look, my dear, what could happen. Suppose you, by some miracle, came to love me; that we agreed to marry. At first, your mother would be stricken by the idea. She would seem to be ill and would be hurt every time you gave up a moment of your time to be with me. But later on, when it came near to the wedding day, there would be so much to do, so much fun for her if she were only up and well again. She will want to be well and then you could do so much to help. You see, you would need her advice, her help and it would be a reversal of your roles. She would be needed by you.'

'And afterwards? How could I ask her to live alone? I couldn't do it!'

'Nor need you. If she were well and active, she could live with us. A doctor's house is always a busy one. If you were to be my secrctary, answer the phone, write my letters, help me, your mother could fulfil a very useful job running the house for us. If she were ill, then it would be an added burden on you and that would be hard for us all. She'd see this and this, too, would help her to get well.'

Alison gave an uncertain smile.

'It seems you have got it all worked out,' she said.

Michael put his hands on her shoulders and looked deep into her green eyes.

'Dreamed out, darling! Do you think I have dared to dream? I thought you hated me; I never believed you could love me. Only now, as I held you in my arms, did it seem possible that you might care a little. Tell me that you do!'

'I don't know, I don't know!' Alison cried truthfully. 'When you look at me like that, I feel – oh, I don't know what it is I feel. I'm so confused. All you've said about Mother and talking about the future . . . everything in my world seems to have turned upside down. Now, this – you – seems to be all that is real. Yet I am afraid that when I get home, this will become a dream and I'll know I was crazy!'

'You do care!' Michael cried in a bright glow of happiness. 'It's only when you are in love that the world seems mad. I'm going to take you home; let you have time to think and sort yourself out. I'm not afraid now. Something in your voice, your eyes, your expression, tells me you've changed completely. You look so very beautiful, my dearest; your eyes are shining and there is a soft glow about you which is like a radiance. Let me kiss you once more.'

Obediently, she lifted her face to his and once again they clung together. Again it was Michael to draw himself away first, knowing that he must at all costs protect her from herself. How incredibly innocent she was. In her new delight in loving, she gave herself to him with complete abandon and a wild passion which thrilled and yet frightened him, too. Such a temperament as hers could be explosive for he, too, was a person with a passionate nature. No wonder that together they either quarrelled or loved. Marriage between them must inevitably be tempestuous, but at the same time what heights and depths they would share.

Alison's thoughts were not so different as he drove her home, yet as they reached the familiar streets her heart grew uncertain and afraid once more. How could she make Bob understand that the newly made engagement must be broken? How could she expect her mother to understand this new strange love for Michael Boyce when she did not even understand it herself? How could she make her mother accept Michael and, not least of all, had she the courage or the belief in Michael's theories to put them into practice?

Six

'It isn't fair to Bob. I don't know what has come over you, Alison.'

Mrs Craig leant back against her pillows, her heart thudding disturbingly in her chest. Alison's abrupt entry into her room and her even more abrupt announcement that she wasn't going to marry Bob after all had been quite a shock. A hundred questions soared through her mind as she noted the change in her daughter. It wasn't just her appearance, although that in itself had altered. The girl's cheeks were glowing and there was a radiance about her that could not be ignored. It was her manner, too.

Alison tried to calm herself. She knew that this conversation with her mother was desperately important. She must be tactful and sensible and level-headed, otherwise her mother might dismiss everything she said as nonsense.

She sat down on the edge of the bed and folded her hands in her lap.

'Mother, I don't honestly believe Bob is in love with me – not *really* in love. And I *know* I'm not in love with him. We couldn't get married not loving each other, could we?'

Mrs Craig's eyes narrowed.

'Not in love with you? That's nonsense. Bob has loved you for years.'

'Yes, but it's a different kind of love!' Alison retorted swiftly. 'We're more like brother and sister.'

'Different!' Mrs Craig repeated the key word on a rising note of anxiety. 'Different from what? Alison, I demand to know what has happened to you. Where have you been these last two hours? You haven't been shopping – and Bob was here just now. He said he'd seen you getting into someone's car.'

Alison paused. So Bob had seen her. Anyway, there was no point in trying to pretend she had not been with Michael.

'Yes, Mother! I only told you I was going shopping as I didn't want you to worry. I went to meet Micahel Boyce. I went to tell him about my engagement to Bob and to tell him I didn't want to see him again.'

Mrs Craig drew in her breath.

'Well, that's one good thing, anyway. I never liked that young man and I never would. Though why you had to see him to tell him that I don't know. I should have thought a telephone call would have sufficed.'

Alison's cheeks were now white. This wasn't going to be easy.

'Michael – he's in love with me!' she blurted out. 'And I think I'm in love with him.' She looked up at her mother's face and seeing there only incredulity and horror, she leant forward in a sudden desperate appeal for understanding, advice, sympathy.

'Please, please don't say anything, not until I've finished. It's all so confusing. You see, I thought I hated him. But I didn't, at least I don't any more. He's really very nice, Mother. I know you'd like him, too, once you got to know him better.'

Mrs Craig's face was now white with sudden fear. There was no possible reason to doubt that Alison had fallen in love. Every line of her face and body suggested a new gentleness, softness, radiance. Once she too had felt like this. Mrs Craig's mouth twisted into a bitter line. Death had brought an end to love, and now Alison, too, would be leaving her. She would be alone...

'Mother, don't look like that! Nothing dreadful has happened.' Alison pleaded, filled with sudden anguish at the expression on her mother's face. 'Don't you see, life is going to be quite different for us now? We won't be alone any more. Michael wants to marry me, take care of me – of us both!'

As the words tumbled from her lips, she knew with a

strange brief certainty that this was what she wanted more than anything in the world. She knew that Michael had been right when he said her life until now had been empty, barren. Now, with him, it was transformed. The future seemed filled with promise, excitement, companionship, love. It was an end to loneliness, to the solitary existence that until today she had accepted as inevitable.

'That man!' Mrs Craig's voice was filled with dislike. 'You must be mad, Alison! I'll never tolerate him for my son-in-law . . . never! And what do you know about him anyway? Nothing at all. I'll never give my consent to this!'

Alison's heart missed a beat. Her mother's antagonism to Michael only served to increase her certainty that she did love him. Hot words of defence of him rushed to her lips but she quenched them quickly, knowing that at all costs she must be tactful. Her mother must be won over to their side. Never, never would Alison quarrel with her.

'Darling Mother!' she said gently. 'You mustn't be prejudiced against him because I am going to marry him, but not now, not right away. You were right when you said I don't know him well; it's true. But we're going to see much more of each other, find out more about each other. And you, too. You'll grow to like him, I know you will. He wants to come and see you.'

'He won't come through this door!' Mrs Craig burst out, but seeing the sudden stubborn tightening of Alison's mouth she realized that this was not, after all, the way to bring Alison to her senses. With a little cry she fell back against her pillow, gasping.

'Mother! Are you all right?'

Alison's instant concern was as automatic as her action to dart forward and hand her mother one of the pills from the box by the bed. But even as she held it out Michael's words came back to her with frightening clarity.

'Whenever things don't go the way your mother wants she will use her illness to achieve her ends.'

Was this an example?

Nothing will make me give Michael up! she thought as

she smoothed her mother's pillow and put back the glass of water on the bedside table.

'Oh, I feel so ill. I think you had better phone Dr McFaddon. I know there's a bad attack coming on.'

'I'm afraid you are upset by my news!' Alison said quietly. 'I ought not to have told you this way. It's been a shock. I'll leave you to rest and we'll discuss it some other time.'

Mrs Craig sat up quickly.

'No, we can't leave things like this. You've got to see sense, Alison. Oh, if only your father were here. How can I, ill as I am, deal with you when you're obviously out of your mind?'

Alison tried to keep calm.

'Mother, I'm not mad. It's all quite simple. I've fallen in love, and the man I'm in love with is a perfectly ordinary and suitable young man. You've no reason to object to him. He isn't married. He has a good job and he's in a very respectable profession. He isn't miles too old or years too young for me. In fact any parent ought to be proud of such a "catch" for her daughter.'

Mrs Craig gave an angry little cry.

'How you can joke about this, I don't know!'

'I'm not joking. I just want you to see it in its right perspective. It isn't the end of the world. I'm not even engaged to Michael yet! Please, Mother, for my sake, be reasonable. See Michael, talk to him. You'll find him as nice as I do if you'll only let yourself.'

'You allow yourself to care for a man who holds the opinion he does of *me*?'

'Mother, Michael told me today that he believed you suffered a great deal. He believes he can help you. He believes he can make you well again. Think how wonderful that would be. There'll be so much to do. You'd like me to have a white wedding, wouldn't you? We could choose my trousseau together. What fun that would be. And afterwards – after we were married – you could help me keep house for Michael. Mother, you do *want* to be well, don't you?'

'You think this. . .this upstart of a young man can perform

58

miracles where an experienced doctor like McFaddon has failed? He really has cast a spell over you, Alison. I'm going to talk to Dr McFaddon about this. The sooner he gets rid of that young quack the better for his practice, I say.'

Alison stood up, suddenly appalled by the venom in her mother's voice. And it was so unfair! She hardly knew Michael.

'We'll talk about it another time!' she said with controlled quietness. 'And don't try to get Dr McFaddon to send Michael away. Because, although I doubt you'd succeed, if you did I'd go with him.'

She walked out of the room, closing the door gently behind her. As she did so she heard her mother burst into hysterical tears. She paused on the landing, torn with the desire to go back into the room and comfort her. She couldn't bear to hear her upset and unhappy. Yet to do so would mean to deny her own future. She couldn't do it. She couldn't give Michael up − not now.

I am in love . . . really in love! she thought. Oh, Michael, Michael! I wish you were here now. I need you badly.

As if in telepathic understanding of her need, the phone suddenly rang and Alison, bounding down the remaining stairs to the hall, knew even before she lifted the receiver that it was him.

'Alison?'

For a moment, she couldn't reply.

'Alison, is that you?'

'Yes!' The word was almost a whisper.

'Are you all right? You sound odd.'

She smiled.

'No, I'm all right. I'm . . . I'm so glad you rang.'

'*Darling!*' The word was like a caress. 'You've no idea how happy it makes me to hear you say that. Are you alone? Can you talk to me?'

'Yes to both questions.'

'Then tell me you love me − you didn't, you know. Until you actually say it, I shan't be able to do a stroke of work!'

She closed her eyes, feeling him near her, knowing that even the sound of his deep soft voice was sufficient to set every nerve in her body alight.

'I love you!' The words were said and hung for a moment on the wire between them.

'Oh, Alison! You said it as if you really meant it, too. You're going to marry me, aren't you?'

'Yes, yes! But not yet, Michael. Mother hasn't taken the news too well. She's terribly upset.'

'Of course, my darling, that was bound to happen. Don't worry. We'll give her plenty of time to get used to the idea. She will, you know, provided you don't weaken. Once she knows your mind is made up and can't be changed, she will have to accept it.'

'It seems so cruel, somehow!' Alison said.

'Don't let it make you unhappy. Remember that in the end this is right for her, too. It has to be this way. Darling, when can I see you? When can I see her?'

'I don't know!' Alison said. 'She won't consider meeting you at the moment.'

'Well, let me come and see you then, after surgery tonight. Please, darling. I want to see you so much. I want you to tell me you love me and to be able to see your eyes as you say it. Maybe you don't really mean it and you're trying to comfort me so I can get back to some work!'

She laughed.

'Now I've made you laugh. I want you to be happy all the time. Alison, I'm coming round about eight.'

'All right!' she said meekly.

'All right, *darling*.'

She smiled again.

'All right, darling!' she repeated obediently.

'I love you!'

'And I love you, too.'

She replaced the receiver and stood by the phone, her heart aglow with intense happiness. This, indeed, must be love. For the first time in her life, she was really and truly in love. This morning she hadn't even known what the word meant.

60

How strange life was! Yet Michael had known from the first that he loved her.

She glanced down at her watch and gave a little cry of surprise. Five o'clock, and she hadn't thought about tea. Yet she wasn't in the least hungry. She must be in love!

Suddenly she remembered Bob. Maybe he would come round after tea. And she didn't want to see him. She didn't want him here this evening at all costs. She would have to ring him up, explain. But the thought of the hurt she might be inflicting on him made the deed thoroughly distasteful to her. Even if he did not love her in the same way Michael did, at least he believed he cared. And Bob was such a dear! It would be a shock, even though she doubted now his heart would be broken.

Michael's phone call had given her new strength, fresh resolve. While his voice was still fresh in her mind she picked up the receiver and dialled Bob's number.

It was Julie who answered.

'I'm afraid Bob's out!' Julie said. 'Is it important?'

'It is, rather. Do you know where he went?'

'To the pictures, I think. He came home in a very bad mood about three, grunted something about Marilyn Monroe on the local and went out again. Any message, Alison?'

'No! Yes! Julie, will you tell Bob not to come round later? Tell him I can't see him – that I'll be writing to him.'

Young as she was Julie guessed from Alison's disjointed sentences, and from her tone of voice, that this was no ordinary message.

'Anything wrong, Alison? It's not your mother?'

'No! Look, Julie, I hate having to say this, but you'll have to know sooner or later and I'm afraid Bob is going to be upset. It's just that – well, I can't marry him after all. Don't tell him that. I'll write and explain. I'd rather he heard from me.'

Julie whistled.

'Golly!' she said childishly. 'Poor old Bob!'

'I know! I feel awful about it, Julie, after all these years. But . . . well, I just don't love him – not the right way.'

61

'I always knew that!' retorted the sixteen-year-old calmly. 'Any fool could have told you that. If you ask me, Bob's known for years you didn't really care for him the way a woman does when she's in love. He just hasn't wanted to admit it to himself. It's made him pretty miserable, too. Not that I'm blaming you, Alison. I suppose you've met someone else?'

'Yes, yes, I have!' Alison said, unaware that her tone of voice had changed even as her thoughts turned to Michael. 'I've fallen properly in love this time! I'm awfully sorry, Julie. I do hope Bob won't mind too much.'

'He'll get over it!' Julie said with sisterly indifference. 'Anyway, better now than after you were married. Good luck, Alison. Ask me to the wedding!'

Julie's attitude was comforting. At least she didn't seem to think her brother would be broken-hearted. He'd find someone else – someone who loved him the way she loved Michael!

Hurriedly, she went along to the kitchen and prepared a tea-tray which she took up to her mother's room. Mrs Craig had stopped crying and was lying against the pillows, her eyes shut.

'Are you asleep, Mother?' Alison asked gently. 'I've brought your tea!'

'I don't want anything to eat. I couldn't possibly keep any food down me!' Mrs Craig murmured.

'Darling!' Alison put down the tray and gently helped her mother into a sitting position. 'At least have a cup of tea!'

'Alison! Tell me it isn't true! Tell me you were just trying to frighten me?'

Mrs Craig's hands were holding fast to hers and Alison felt their tenacious grip with a sudden chill in her heart. How difficult it was to be strong when you felt so desperately sorry for someone, when you had loved them and cared for them and protected them for so long.

'Please, Mother! Won't you try to be happy about it for my sake? I couldn't help falling in love with Michael. In fact, I know now that I fought against it ever since our first

62

meeting. Now it has happened and nothing can change it – nothing. I can never stop loving him. And he loves me: I'd be so terribly happy if only you were happy, too.'

Mrs Craig looked at her daughter with fear clutching again at her heart, making it pound so fiercely that she did indeed feel ill.

'I would be happy for you, Alison, if I thought you were in love with the *right man*. You know how pleased I was when you told me you were engaged to Bob. I've always liked him, always been happy in my mind about the thought that one day you two would get married. This love you say you feel for the new doctor...can't you see it isn't anything more than infatuation? I want to protect you from getting hurt. You *think* you love him because you find him, no doubt, attractive. I'll grant he is very good-looking. But all the more reason not to trust him, Alison, or yourself.'

'But that's unreasonable. I'll admit I'm very much attracted to him, but it isn't that only. It's something deep down here.' She placed her hand over her heart. 'Don't ask me how I know, Mother. I just do know I'm in love, really in love. I never felt this way about Bob and now I could never marry Bob. It's Michael or no one.'

'Better you should never get married than marry the wrong man!' Mrs Craig replied swiftly.

'But he isn't the wrong man. And we're not getting married tomorrow, or next week, maybe not even this year!' Alison protested. 'We'll have as long as we need to get to know each other better, to be *sure*.'

'You'll regret this!' Mrs Craig vowed. 'I know this isn't the way. How long have you known him? A few weeks! It's obvious to anyone but a fool that you're infatuated. I've no doubt a man like that knows just the way to turn a young girl's head. Watch out, Alison!'

Alison bit her lip, struggling not to answer back in anger.

'Tell me any one thing against Michael you know to his discredit?' she said quietly. 'You can't, Mother. He isn't the villain you'd like me to believe him. He's just an ordinary, nice young doctor. Dr McFaddon thinks the world of him.'

'He's far too good-looking!' Mrs Craig said. 'I'd never trust a man like that. Why isn't he married already? He must be in his thirties! Don't tell me he hasn't had girls after him with looks like that. And I've no doubt he knows full well how to take what he wants and avoid the responsibilities of marriage.'

'That's unfair and horrible!' Alison burst out. 'I'm not going to listen to that kind of talk. And you won't put me against him that way. He's coming to see me this evening. If you'd like to talk to him, then I'll bring him up.'

'He's not coming into my house!' Mrs Craig cried, her face now suffused with anger.

'It's my house, too, Mother. I work hard to help us keep it going. I think I'm entitled to entertain my friends in it.'

Mrs Craig burst into tears.

'You've changed!' she wept bitterly. 'You don't care about anything any more except this man! You're taking advantage of the fact that I'm ill and not fit to look after you. If I were well, you wouldn't dare defy me this way.'

'Oh, Mother!' Alison said despairingly. 'Can't you understand that I don't want to defy you? I want us to be friends, all of us. I'm not a child any longer. I'm twenty-one and it's time I had a life of my own. It isn't selfish to want to marry someone you love, is it? You don't want me to give up thoughts of marriage and children?'

'I'm not going to talk about it any more!' Mrs Craig replied on another sob. 'I feel far too ill.'

Michael is right! Alison thought. Whenever it suits her, she is ill. But I mustn't be angry with her. He said to be gentle and understanding.

Quietly she removed the untouched tea-tray and once more left her mother alone.

Seven

In the surgery the last patient had left and Diane was tidying the room. Michael was hurriedly clearing his desk, his eye on the clock. He wanted time to go back to his digs and change before going to Alison's house.

The thought of Alison was like an intoxication. It was only from sheer habit that he had been able to concentrate on his work. Now it was seven fifteen and in three-quarters of an hour he would be with her!

Diane Fellows looked at him speculatively from across the room. She had sensed with that peculiar feminine instinct of hers that there was something different about Michael tonight; a suppressed excitement, even a gaiety one might call it. Certainly she had never seen him in this mood before.

'Feel like another drink?' she asked casually.

'Um?' Michael looked up, only half-concentrating on her words. 'Oh, no, not this evening, thanks all the same, Nurse.'

'Diane!' she said sharply. 'I'm off duty now, you know!'

Michael grinned back.

'OK, Diane!'

'Anything special on?' Diane asked lightly.

'Special? Does it show that bad?' Michael gave a a boyish, happy laugh. 'Look, I'll let you into a secret, Diane. I must tell someone or burst. It's Alison. Alison Craig. We're in love! Does that sound awfully silly?'

To Diane it didn't sound silly but it shocked her so completely that she only just managed to control the swift words of protest that rushed to her lips. Michael, in love with Alison Craig! No, it couldn't be. Michael was hers,

65

hers. No silly young girl was going to take him away from her.

'In love?' she said quietly, an enigmatic smile on her face. 'That sounds – well – improbable, coming from you, Michael. And especially with a girl like Alison Craig!'

He glanced at her questioningly, slightly irritated now by her words with their implied criticism of Alison.

'And why not?'

Diane turned away and idly picked up a magazine.

'Oh, I don't know! I should have thought she wasn't quite your type. She's so young, so inexperienced. I would have thought her sort bored you!'

Michael gave a little shout of laughter.

'Alison, boring? You just don't know her, Diane. Underneath that quiet exterior, she's vital and alive. That mother of hers has done her best to squash her temperament, but it's there, Diane.'

'I thought that you two didn't get on too well!' Diane murmured. 'Last time she was here—'

'Oh, that was only a misunderstanding about her mother. The woman's a hypochondriac of the first order. Alison naturally objected to my saying so. Now she understands and everything's all right between us.'

'I see!' Diane looked at his glowing, happy face and knew a violent and completely basic jealousy of the girl who could bring that look to Michael's face. In that instant she could have killed Alison; how could she dare to sneak Michael away from beneath her grasp! For Michael would have fallen for her if it hadn't been for Miss Craig! Constant proximity, suggestion, loneliness, the flat – it would all have worked out right. And now Alison had beaten her to the post. Yes, she could kill her! But there were other ways.

'I hope you'll be happy,' she said coolly.

'You don't sound as if you think we will!' Michael replied laughing, unaffected by her disapproval.

'I don't want to be a wet blanket, but if you want my honest answer, I don't!' Diane retorted. 'Of course, you know the set-up better than I do, but in my opinion that mother of hers has a far greater hold over her than you imagine. Right now, when she really believes herself in love with you, no doubt Mother takes a back seat. But you wait a while. I doubt if Alison has the strength of character to fight that woman.'

'I can do the fighting for both of us!' Michael said confidently. 'Well, I must push off. I want to get back to my digs and change before I go out. See you tomorrow, Diane!'

He walked out and left her staring after him through narrowed eyes. If he had turned to see her expression, he might have guessed something of the raging jealousy that tore through her. Frustration, anger, bitterness and venom – all were in the long, hazel eyes. And determination, too. At least she, Diane, did not suffer from scruples. She would fight Alison for him, fight her with every weapon she knew, fair or unfair. Alison might be winning now, but she wouldn't win in the end.

Happily ignorant of her thoughts, Michael knocked on the door of Alison's house half an hour later, and in an instant she was in his arms, her mouth pressed against his own in a glad welcome.

He held her for a long moment, radiantly happy in her unselfconscious show of love for him. He had no need to doubt her now. Her eyes, cheeks, her whole body was aglow and her love shone only and transparently for him to see.

'Oh, Alison!' he whispered, kicking the door shut behind him and taking her once more into his arms in the darkness of the hall. 'It seems like a hundred years since the afternoon, and it's really only a few hours. Soon I shan't be able to bear even a minute away from you!'

She smiled happily, her hand caressing the back of his head.

'I love you, I love you, I love you!' she whispered.

'And I love you, my darling!' he said against the sweet softness of her mouth.

Presently, Alison broke away from him, holding his hand tightly and drawing him into the sitting-room where a bright fire glowed. He looked at her fully then and to his eyes she

67

was even more lovely than he remembered her. She was in slacks now, outlining her long slim legs. Over them she was wearing a soft fluffy V-necked jersey, white and loose fitting yet clinging to her small pointed breasts, stirring him to an intense desire for her.

He sat down in the nearest armchair, pulling her on to his lap where she sat with her arms twined about his neck.

'You're so beautiful!' he said, kissing her eyes, her mouth, her neck and the soft creamy skin that the jersey she wore did not cover.

She stirred in his arms, her body trembling beneath his touch, every nerve seeming to jump alive with a new and painful longing for him. She looked at him, studying for the first time his brown eyes, the way his brows grew so surprisingly dark above them, then traced with her finger the strong line of his cheek and jaw and then, with her fingertips, his mouth.

He caught her hand and pressed his lips against it, fighting against the desire in him, afraid to frighten her with his longing for her. He must not forget that love was new to her, that unlike her contemporaries she was inexperienced with sex. He must protect her from herself as well as from himself.

'I want to make love to you, properly!' he whispered, his face now against the softness of her hair.

'I know!' Alison said shyly. 'I want it, too. Michael, it isn't going to be easy, is it? I know now what you mean about love being pain, too. Loving you like this hurts.'

'But it is beautiful, too!' Michael replied.

She nodded.

'Michael, Mother won't accept you. She thinks that it's all infatuation, physical attraction. She thinks that sex is all you want from me.'

Michael sat up, placing his two hands either side of her face so that she must look directly into his eyes.

'No, it isn't all!' he said harshly. 'I want you, yes! More than I've ever wanted a woman in my life. But even if you were to offer me what I wanted now, Alison, I wouldn't take

68

it. I love you. Not just your body. I want you for my wife. I want to be able to share my life with you, take care of you, make you happy. I want you to bear my children and for us to share them. I love you, darling, with my whole heart!'

She smiled, completely content with his reply, and gratefully touched his mouth in a light kiss.

'It's how I feel about you, Michael. Mother doesn't understand. She doesn't *want* to like you. I've had a terrible time with her!'

'I'm sorry!' Michael said. 'Don't you think she might feel differently if I could see her, talk to her?'

'She refuses to see you! She tried to forbid me letting you come here to the house. Michael, she can't stop me seeing you.'

'No, darling, she can't! But we don't want to be permanently in opposition to her, do we? It can't be easy or nice for you. Let's give her a little while to get used to the idea and then we'll contrive some way for me to see her. I'm sure if we did I could convince her my intentions are strictly honourable!'

Alison gave a happy little laugh. Here, like this, in Michael's arms, there seemed no reason to fear the future. He could take care of everything, smooth out the difficulties. She felt a complete and wonderful relaxation of responsibility. For so long she had had to bear the responsibilities for herself and her mother. Now Michael was lifting a great weight from her shoulders.

'I love you!' she cried, the words springing up from deep within her.

'And I love you!' Michael said, but afraid now of the intensity of the moment, he pushed her gently away from him and said with forced lightness:

'What about something to eat, darling? If I'm going to marry you, I must find out first if you can cook!'

Alison laughed and jumped to her feet.

'The way to a man's heart. But it's only curry, I'm afraid. You didn't give me enough warning you were coming or I'd have cooked a banquet. Sit down, darling, and I'll go and get it. We can have it on a tray here in front of the fire.'

She was gone only a very little while. He heard her go upstairs first, go into Mrs Craig's room. For a moment, he heard the older woman's voice, raised in anger. Then the door closed quietly and Alison came into the room.

They ate quickly and without speaking, except when Michael congratulated her on the curry. Then she gave him only a half-smile. It wasn't until she had brought in the coffee that he realized something was wrong. The happiness had gone from her face.

'What was it, darling? What's the matter?'

Alison turned to him in sudden despair.

'It's Mother. She said if you weren't out of the house in half an hour she would ring Dr McFaddon.'

'Dr McFaddon? But why?'

'To say . . . to say—' She broke off, suddenly near to tears. Michael took her hands and pulled them away from her face.

'Tell me, Alison! It can't be as bad as all that!'

'It is – it's horrible! She said she'd tell Dr McFaddon you were—'

'Making love to you? Raping you?' Michael's voice was calm and quiet. 'Sweetheart, she won't do any such thing. And even if she did, Doc wouldn't believe a word of it. He knows me too well!'

'I said he'd never believe her. Mother said then she would ring the police.'

'Darling, don't let it upset you! She won't. These are just threats. She has to try to make you give me up. I didn't expect anything else. You must remember that it isn't easy for her letting you go. Be calm and patient. Don't let her see you are frightened.'

'It wasn't so much the threats, although I was afraid. I know a doctor has to be careful of his reputation! But she looks so ill, Michael, and I've never known her to be so unreasonable. You don't think that worry about us could really make her ill? If I thought she was really ill I – I couldn't fight her, Michael.'

'Look, Alison, you can go to Dr McFaddon and ask him

70

outright for the truth if you don't trust my diagnosis. I would like you to do so.'

'It isn't that I doubt *you*, Michael, but how can anyone, any doctor, be sure about things like this? I know everything points to you being right. Today, when I told her about us, and when I really put my foot down, she said she felt ill. But it could be true, too, that she really does feel ill. You said yourself people can suffer from imaginary illness.'

'You're getting confused, Alison. Let's take it in easy stages. First, is your mother genuinely ill? My answer to that is she has no chronic illness. She is, in a way, ill in her mind. Now, if she has an imaginary illness, does she suffer and become really ill? The answer to that must be yes. But giving way to her won't make her better. You *must* be firm, darling, for all our sakes. For hers just as much as ours.'

Alison relaxed. Deep down inside, she felt Michael was right. Besides, she couldn't go back to the old life now. Nothing could ever be ordinary and quiet and normal again. The rut she had lived in had seemed quite bearable until Michael had shown her the unlimited horizon above. There was no going back. Everything that was ardent and passionate in her nature demanded the rich fullness of life with the man she loved.

Suddenly, shrilly, the telephone rang. It was unexpected for it seldom rang in this house.

Bob! she thought. She didn't want to talk to him, not now. Her letter to him explaining everything lay on the hall table ready for posting. The last thing she wished was to have to explain over the telephone.

'I shan't answer it!' she said.

Michael smiled.

'You'll have to cure yourself of the habit of ignoring phone calls in the future, dearest. It rings non-stop in a doctor's house.'

'It couldn't be for you, could it?' Alison asked, jumping up. 'Does anyone know you are here?'

'Yes. Better see, Alison. My night for emergency calls so I left your number with Dr McFaddon.'

71

Obediently Alison went to the phone and returned a moment later.

'It's someone called Mrs Fellows, Mrs Diane Fellows. She's had an accident and wanted to know if you could go round right away. Michael, that isn't the nurse, is it?'

Michael frowned in annoyance. Of all the bad luck! He'd so looked forward to these few hours alone with Alison.

'Is she on the line?'

'No, she just said to go round. Will you have to go?'

'Yes, darling!' Michael said, happy at her reluctance for him to leave. 'Diane's a nurse and she wouldn't call me unless it was serious. She didn't say what had happened?'

'No, she didn't!'

Alison watched him pull on his overcoat and as he turned to kiss her goodbye she flung her arms round him.

'I love you so much!' she whispered as he kissed her.

He pulled himself away, knowing that he must leave quickly or he would never have the strength of will to leave at all.

'I'll ring you tomorrow,' he promised.

Once away from Alison's house, Michael's mind turned to the problem in hand. It was after ten o'clock. What on earth had happened to Diane? He knew it was unfair, but he felt full of irritation with her. If she'd had a fall or hurt herself why hadn't she called an ambulance? It had better be serious or he would have her over the coals for calling him out for nothing.

He reached Diane's flat and rang the bell. She must have been watching for him for a moment later the door opened. She was wearing a dressing-gown, ice-blue in colour which accentuated the dead-white of her skin. He saw at a glance that her lower arm was heavily bandaged. Bright-pink stains had seeped through in places.

'What on earth happened?' he asked, thoroughly the doctor now and anxious about her. She looked so deathly pale and she was trembling violently.

'Cut myself!' she said briefly. 'Sorry to drag you out so late. It was fortunate I knew where to find you.'

72

He followed her into the kitchen where a bowl of disinfectant lay on the table together with bandages and lint. She had obviously given herself first-aid.

'I don't seem to be able to stop the bleeding,' she said as he unwound the bandage.

There was an ugly, jagged cut across her wrist. Michael looked at it and said sharply:

'You'll need a couple of stitches, Diane. Sorry!'

'That's all right. I thought it might!' Diane said. 'Besides, it's my own fault.'

'What did you do? Break a milk bottle or something?' Michael asked as he set to work to cleanse the wound.

Diane Fellows looked at the bent head and knew that the moment had come when she must take the gamble. She had planned this moment so carefully and yet now, suddenly, she knew a moment's fear. Suppose she hadn't judged him right. Suppose he didn't react as she wanted?

Whatever else, Diane was no coward. Half an hour earlier, she had quite coolly and deliberately broken a milk bottle and taking care to avoid the large vein, had cut her wrist. Not too deep, of course, but enough to make the blood flow. It hadn't hurt as she had given herself a local anaesthetic first. It would hurt later, but not much. Not enough to deter her. Then she had rung Alison's Craig's house. Now she must play her hand and her act had better be good.

'What happened?' Michael asked her again.

'I . . . I'd rather not say. I was very stupid!' Diane's voice was husky and hesitant. Glancing at her quickly, Michael saw her eyes drop beneath his gaze. What made her hesitate to tell him about the accident? Surely she couldn't be afraid of admitting to a moment's carelessness. Or was it something more?

'I'll stitch it now. May hurt, I'm afraid.'

She never murmured while he neatly stitched the wound. He admired her for that. As soon as it was freshly bandaged, she went out of the room and came back a moment later with two whiskies.

He didn't really want a drink but it was obvious she needed a stimulant. So he accepted to keep her company.

'Now!' he said, as he took the glass from her. 'Let's have it, Diane.'

She turned away from him and walked over to the window.

'*Please*, don't make me tell you!'

He knew now that something more was wrong. For a moment, he still could not think how such a cut could have been made if not by broken glass. Then, quite suddenly, he knew. Diane had done it deliberatcly.

He was shocked, too shocked to be tactful. His voice sharp, he said:

'You didn't try to cut your wrist?'

Her silence was all the answer he needed. He jumped up and went across to her, pulling her round by the shoulders.

'That's a mad, crazy thing to do, Diane! And you a nurse. Are you out of your mind?'

She gave him a long, desperate look of appeal.

'Please, Michael, don't be cross with me. You don't understand. You couldn't be expected to know how hopeless things have seemed. I know it was mad and I regretted it immediately; it's wrong to take this way out. But I couldn't bear my life any more – I just couldn't!'

The next minute she was leaning against him, her sobs muffled against his shoulder.

Pity for her replaced his first feeling of shock and surprise. Poor kid! She was all alone in the world and just because she controlled her private grief inwardly was no reason to suppose she did not suffer as much as those who could weep openly. More, perhaps. It was always bad to be introverted. She must have touched rock bottom to contemplate killing herself. Thank heaven she had had the sense to stop before it was too late!

Sensing his concern for her, Diane quickly followed up the advantage. How easy it was to fool men. They actually liked to think of one as weak and helpless and dependent. This man had no time at all for the cool, capable and efficient nurse.

74

'Oh, Michael! I've been so lonely!' she whispered between sobs. 'You can't know what it has been like for me since Peter died. Every night I come back here to face another long lonely evening. There's no point in living, that's the dreadful part of it.'

'Nonsense!' Michael said sharply, trying to rally her. Self-pity could be dangerous in this emotional state. Sympathy, too. 'You're young and pretty, Diane. I know you won't want to think about falling in love again, but you will. And you've everything to live for. Think, Diane, how much you have, not how much you have lost. Youth, beauty, independence. There are women by the dozen who would give everything they own to possess so much.'

'It's worth nothing without love!' Diane said. She moved away from him and stood with drooping shoulders by the window. 'I don't expect you to understand. You are a man. I'm a woman and I need something more than a career to live for.'

'I do understand that,' Michael argued. 'But you will fall in love again one day, Diane.'

She turned and looked at him. Was this the right moment? She mustn't undo her present advantage, and yet if she were to consolidate her position she must go on.

'I – I have!' she said quietly. 'That may shock you, Michael, but it's true. When Peter died, I didn't believe I could ever love anyone else, although everyone told me time would change my beliefs. But love takes no account of time. I've fallen in love again and this time it is even more hopeless than the last.'

Michael sat back suddenly on the hard kitchen chair. He felt out of his depth. If it was not grief which had made her want to kill herself, then what was it? A hopeless love affair?

'Better tell me everything, Diane. I'd like to help if I can,' he said genuinely.

'Would you, Michael? I don't really see why I should bore you with my troubles.'

Michael grimaced.

'I'd no idea I'd given you to believe I was such a self-centred person,' he said with an attempt to lighten the conversation. 'Of course I'm interested in you, Diane. And, moreover, I shouldn't have a moment's peace in the future if I thought you could be driven to doing such a terrible thing again.'

Diane appeared to hesitate. Then she said:

'All right! Let's go through into the sitting-room.'

He followed her in, noting as he did so that the little gold clock on the mantelpiece showed half past ten. It was getting late, but he couldn't leave her like this. It would be inhuman.

Diane sat back gracefully in one of the armchairs and Michael seated himself opposite her. He was still wearing his overcoat, but when Diane suggested he should remove it he shook his head.

'No, I mustn't stay too long so there's no point getting too comfortable,' he said. He also refused a drink. Diane poured herself a double brandy and played for time. She *must* go carefully. Scare him off now and there really would be no future. Gently, gently! she told herself. You've done well so far. Go slow!

'Really, Michael, it would only bore you,' she said. 'I know you must be tired. Leave me alone and I'll fight it out by myself. I promise I won't do anything silly again. I guess I'm too much of a coward, anyway. I messed this up well and truly, didn't I?'

Michael frowned.

'No one is ever worth the sacrifice of a human life,' he said sternly. 'No one!'

'All right. I'll accept that!' Diane replied with an enigmatic smile. 'But what is a human life worth, Michael? Mine is worth nothing to me – nothing at all.'

'I can't believe that. You only think that now. It may all sort itself out, Diane, and in the years to come, you'll be so glad you're alive to enjoy them.'

'Perhaps! But it isn't very likely!' Diane's voice this time held a true ring of bitterness. 'You see, the man I'm in love with is mad about someone else.'

'I'm sorry! Is he married?'

76

Diane shook her head.

'No! But it won't be long now, by the look of things, before he is.'

'And you're sure? That you do really love him? It isn't just a kind of rebound from your husband's death?'

Diane seemed not to take objection to the personal question.

'I'm sure. You see, Michael, my love for Peter was quite different. It was – well, a maternal love. I wanted to take care of him, protect him. But this is a different kind of love. It burns inside me so that I can hardly bear it.'

Her voice throbbed and Michael could not doubt the sincerity of her words now. Her whole body seemed to glow with unsatiated desire. She looked feline, passionate, dangerous and very, very lovely. He wondered how any man in his senses could deny himself such a woman. But quickly, he curbed the thought. He must remain impartial if he was to help her.

'You think it's wrong of me to – to fall in love again so quickly?' Diane was questioning him. 'Can't you see that this is different? While Peter lived I never dreamed of such a love. I was quite content just to adore him. He was so sweet, so kind, so good. But then I met this man. . .a different kind of man altogether. I knew for the first time then what love meant.'

Yes, thought Michael. It can happen that way. Often in the past he had imagined himself in love. He might even have married and gone on deluding himself into thinking what he felt was love. Until he met Alison. Then he'd known an entirely different range of emotions. She had opened up a new world of feeling. He could no more deny its reality than could Diane.

'I do understand!' he said. 'I don't blame you, Diane. It's common knowledge what a wonderful wife you were to your husband. No one could blame you for falling in love again. It's right that you should.'

'But useless!' Diane said flatly. 'He's in love with another girl.'

'Or just believes himself in love with someone else?' Michael questioned hopefully. 'Maybe in time, he'll grow to see you as you really are and then . . .'

'Then you believe I have a right to fight for him?' Diane asked, leaning forward and staring into Michael's face. 'You think I have the right to take him away, from the other girl?'

Michael dropped his eyes. Was it fair? All's fair in love and war, they said, but there was always a loser. Was any woman justified in taking another woman's man from her? If there were no engagement perhaps. He hadn't hesitated to take Alison from Bob, even though they were engaged. But then he'd been so sure she didn't love him.

'I can't answer that,' he said, acknowledging his weakness, his unwillingness to be responsible. 'You see, I've done just that with Alison. She was actually engaged. But then I was sure in my own mind that she didn't love the man.'

'And if I am sure he doesn't love the other girl? That together they couldn't reach the heights that he and I could reach? If I could believe that, there'd be some point in going on. I would fight, too.'

'I can't advise you, Diane. I can only wish you luck in what you decide to do. I think you should be very sure first, of yourself, I mean. It would be such a terrible thing to break up a happy union for something which wasn't going to last.'

Diane gave him a long, slow look from those enigmatic, slanting eyes.

'It would last. It isn't an affair I want, Michael. I want him for keeps.'

'Lucky fellow!' Michael said lightly. He got up and put a hand on her shoulder in a brotherly pat. 'Look, I think you ought to take a couple of days off at least. I'll tell Dr McFaddon you've had a bit of a nervous breakdown. No point in spreading around what you did this evening. Small places like this gossip soon gets about and it's a criminal offence, you know. But we'll look on it as an accident provided I've your promise, your solemn word of honour, you won't do anything like this again?'

78

'I promise! And I don't want time off. Don't you see, more time to be alone, to think, to mope...'

Michael brightened.

'I know, I'll ask Alison to pop along tomorrow and have a chat with you. You'll like her, Diane. She's such a wonderful girl. She'd be company and maybe you two would become good friends. Alison could do with a friend, too. She's spent far too much of her time worrying about that mother of hers.'

Alison Craig! Her friend! How blind men could be. Didn't he know Alison was her enemy, the one who had taken everything Diane wanted? Yet maybe it was not such a bad idea, Alison coming here. Maybe Alison, knowing the truth, would step out of the picture and leave the field free for her. Maybe...

'I'd love that, Michael,' she said, jumping to her feet and now seemingly back on an even keel again emotionally. 'And, Michael, thank you for coming, for saving my life, for being so nice.'

Before he realized what she intended to do, she bent forward and kissed him swiftly on the lips. He did not return the kiss, too surprised by its unexpectedness to avoid it. Just her unaffected and rather charming way of expressing her thanks he told himself as he bade her goodnight and quickly walked out to his car. A strange and fascinating woman. Funny how for so long he'd only thought of her as Nurse Fellows, not as a woman at all.

He was suddenly very tired. When he reached his digs he thought for a moment of ringing Alison, just to hear her voice, to say goodnight, but then he stopped himself. It was past eleven and she would probably be in bed asleep.

Surprisingly, he had barely climbed into bed before he, too, fell into a dreamless sleep.

Eight

D iane lay on the sofa, her bandaged arm across the back, her long slim legs crossed gracefully. She had taken great time and trouble with her appearance, wanting at this first meeting with Alison to have the upper hand by making the younger girl feel unsophisticated and immature.

She had succeeded. Alison was all too conscious of her dull, shapeless skirt when she had seen Diane's green troubadour trousers; of the hand-knitted blue jersey when she saw Diane's expensive matching suede gilet. She hadn't really wanted to come at all, but Michael had been so pressing.

'Please, darling! She needs someone so badly.'

He had rung her after breakfast to tell her what had happened last night. Of course, he hadn't told her everything, only that Diane had been in a desperate frame of mind and that he was worried about her. Seeing the bandaged wrist as she came into Diane's flat, Alison had put two and two together.

She felt quite inadequate to deal with someone like Diane. After all, what could she do? Everything about this woman was strange and unfamiliar to her. Yet Michael had believed she could help. To please him she must try. If only she could like Diane or feel sorry for her! Knowing she had tried to kill herself didn't help. Somehow Alison could not believe that this self-possessed, beautifully made-up and poised woman could have been suicidal only last night.

It was mid-morning: Mrs Craig believed her daughter had gone shopping. Alison, hating the deceit, had nevertheless avoided a scene by letting her mother go on thinking she was going to the chemist. Later, after lunch, she was meeting

Michael. She did so want to be able to report to him that she had helped Diane, but how?

It was Diane who opened the conversation after the preliminary awkwardness had been got over.

'I hear you and Michael are madly in love?' she said, stressing the word 'madly' so that to Alison it sounded almost sarcastic. She was furious with herself for blushing.

'We . . . yes, we are!' she stammered.

'Then I must congratulate you. I suppose your family are delighted to welcome a doctor as a future son-in-law?'

'I have no family – that is, only my mother. I'm afraid she doesn't take too kindly to the idea. You see, she is naturally afraid of losing me. We've been very close since my father died.'

Diane knew she had played her first card right.

'That must be very upsetting for you,' she said. 'I can see how much you must hate the idea of upsetting her. At the same time, one can see her point of view, too.'

Alison warmed to the understanding and sympathy in Diane's voice.

'I think it's hard, too, on Michael. Poor darling, he hasn't exactly had a welcome into the home. Mother refuses even to see him. But he's wonderfully patient and understanding I'm *sure* it will be all right once Mother gets to know him. He's such a wonderful person.'

'Yes, I know. No one could have been sweeter last night, or so understanding. He's a truly good person – and I believe he'll go a long way. You must be very proud that he loves you.'

Alison flushed.

'Yes, I am! It still doesn't seem real. I expect it sounds silly to you, but I began by hating him. I think it was really because I objected to the way he behaved about Mother.'

'Tell me!' Diane commanded.

Alison fell into the trap. Diane concealed her own growing confidence. This was going to be so much easier than she had hoped. Already she had a valuable ally in Mrs Craig, and what a strong ally, too! Duty would die hard in a girl like Alison. Clearly duty had been the governing factor of her whole adult life.

'Of course, one can see Michael's point of view!' Diane said quietly, when Alison had finished her account of her various meetings with Michael. 'Naturally it must have been exasperating for him to have you put your mother first. But one wonders altogether if he *is* right. I mean, you do owe your mother a lot, don't you? And she is so completely dependent on you!'

'Yes, I know!' Alison said. 'But ever since Michael explained that it's best for Mother in the long run, I've been able to be firm with her. Michael says she isn't really ill at all. So long as I'm sure of that, I can stand up to her.'

'But how can he be so sure there isn't anything wrong? Has she been examined, by a specialist, I mean?'

'No!' Alison admitted. 'But Michael hasn't any doubt at all.'

Diane raised her eyesbrows.

'I'd have thought that a bit rash. After all, as a nurse I know only too well that doctors aren't infallible. They can be wrong. Not, of course, that I think Michael is wrong necessarily. But it isn't always so easy to diagnose illness even these days. Even specialists make mistakes. Think how often you read in the papers about people who've only just had a check-up at hospital and the next day are dead! Frankly, I don't trust anyone. I suppose I know too much about it for my own peace of mind!'

Skilfully, she had succeeded in planting the first seed of doubt in Alison's mind. Was Michael wrong? It would be too awful if her mother were genuinely suffering and she adding to her pain by being remote and entirely selfish about her love for Michael.

'No!' Alison said quickly. 'I'm sure Michael knows what he is talking about. He convinced me absolutely. And once I'd been made to understand Mother's state of mind, every-thing fits into place. I've noticed already how she is feeling worse when things go wrong for her.'

'But that is natural,' Diane said easily. 'One has only to

be desperately unhappy to feel ill. It's to do with the nervous system . . . tension, that kind of thing. And when one is happy, then the aches and pains have a miraculous way of disappearing.'

Alison smiled.

'Yes, I know! Since I've been in love with Michael I've been too happy to think about headaches or anything else.' Suddenly she remembered the reason for her visit. Ashamed, she said quickly:

'Michael told me you'd had a kind of breakdown. I do wish there was something I could do.'

It would be easier if Diane looked as if she were a nervous wreck, but she did not. She looked cool, calm, completely in her right mind.

'No one can help me but myself!' Diane replied. 'Michael made me see that last night. I suppose he told you I tried to kill myself?'

Alison dropped her eyes. She couldn't bear to hear those words, so harsh and terrible in the warm feminine comfort of Diane's sitting-room. They seemed so out of place, so wrong.

'Michael didn't tell me. I . . . I guessed. Diane, how *could* you? It's a terrible thing to do.'

Diane laughed, a bitter laugh without humour.

'How easy for you to condemn me from the height of your happiness! Can you have any idea of the misery others suffer? No, you've led a sheltered, protected life. I was married to a man who, for years, was slowly dying despite everything I could do for him. Can you imagine what that was like, seeing the man you love die slowly and painfully? And then I fell in love again. And it's just as hopeless as my marriage.'

Alison listened, appalled. In Diane's harsh matter-of-fact voice how terrible life sounded.

'Now I've shocked you!' Diane said, amused. 'Well, no doubt as a doctor's wife, you'll have worse shocks than this. It isn't going to be easy for you, Alison. I wonder if you know that, or if Michael realizes it. A doctor's wife needs to be more than just a woman. She needs to be a tower of strength and patience and be willing to be a slave to his profession just as much as he is.'

'But I don't mind that!' Alison cried. 'I'd do anything for Michael, anything in the world!'

'Kill yourself for love of him?' Diane broke in.

For a moment Alison was silenced. Would she? The very idea was terrible, frightening and yet somewhere, deep down inside, she felt that if anything happened to Michael, she would be glad to die. She wouldn't want to live in a world without him.

'Suppose you have to choose between him and your mother?' Diane forced Alison on through death to something worse.

'No, that couldn't happen. Michael wouldn't let it. He knows how much my mother means to me and how terribly she depends on me. He wouldn't ask me to choose.'

'But your mother might. What then?'

Alison shivered and suddenly shook her shoulders as if to throw away this new burden of thought.

'Don't let's talk about things like that. It couldn't ever happen. I'm so lucky in having found someone like Michael who understands.'

'Yes!'

Diane turned away and stared out of the window. Deep within a kind of cold fury raged. What was there about this girl that attracted Michael so violently? What had she that Diane herself did not possess in equal measure? Alison was attractive, but it wasn't a breathtaking beauty; it wasn't even an irresistible allure. Just an ordinary quota of nice looks and perhaps rather specially lovely eyes. But nothing tremendous. Perhaps it was that shining innocence, that lack of sophistication that attracted him? A look she, Diane, had never had, even in her teens. But she had something more. It had to be more. No man she had wanted had ever refused what she had to offer. How dared Michael! To be shouldered aside by this girl, when she could make Michael's life a heaven – perhaps a hell, too, but a heaven he could never reach with Alison Craig.

She turned to Alison with a careful smile.

'I wonder if I could be of any use?' she mused. 'I know it isn't any of my business, but Michael and you have both been so kind. Perhaps if I were to see your mother? Act as a sort of go-between? Maybe I could make her understand how you feel about each other? She would realize I had no axe to grind.'

Alison's instinctive words of refusal died on her lips. Perhaps it wasn't such a bad idea. Maybe her mother would listen to someone like Diane. Not only was Diane a nurse, but she was someone who knew Michael in his work, who admired and liked him. Maybe she *could* make her mother see reason.

Diane noticed her hesitation and quickly cemented her advantage.

'Let me come this afternoon. I've nothing to do. It'll help me get my mind off my own problems. I daresay you could manage to be out?'

'Oh, yes!' Alison agreed. 'Michael and I—'

'That's settled then,' Diane broke in smoothly. 'You pop off for the afternoon with Michael and I'll drop in casually with some pills or something and stay and chat.'

'You're awfully kind!' Alison said warmly. 'I wish I could do something for you, Diane. Is it. . . I mean, is the man you love . . . won't he marry you?'

'Not as things stand at the moment!' Diane said with another of her enigmatic smiles. 'But today things don't seem so hopeless. I realize I was wrong to try to end my life last night. While there's life there's always hope.'

'Yes, that's true!' Alison cried. 'You must always cling to that thought, Diane, when things look black.'

She stood up and impulsively reached out her hand in a gesture of friendship and goodbye.

'I'm glad we're friends,' she said. 'Promise me you'll tell me if there is ever anything I can do for you.'

Going home through the all but empty streets, Alison knew a strange feeling of happiness. She was so lucky . . . so very lucky. It was wonderful to be in love and to know

the man you loved so much in turn loved you. This afternoon she would be in his arms, feel his mouth on hers, hear
his beloved voice. How terribly empty life would seem
without him. Poor Diane, poor Bob, poor all the people
who had no one to love them. Poor Mother who had lost
her love. Yet the time would come, must come, when her
mother knew real happiness again. With Diane's help, she
would understand and see Michael and grow to love him,
too.

Later, sitting in Michael's car with his arms round her,
his face against her hair, she told him how happy she was
about their future.

'Don't you see, darling, that if Mother can be made to
accept you quickly, we might not have to wait so long before
we can become engaged.'

He pressed his face closer against her, loving her for her
honest admission that she wanted to marry him soon. Half
an hour in each other's arms had been enough to show them
how desperate and urgent was their physical need of each
other. Neither wanted to wait for fulfilment, for the chance
to give and take everything.

'All the same, I don't know if Diane is the right person,'
he said thoughtfully. 'Somehow I can't see her and your
mother understanding one another. Still, I suppose it's worth
a try. Decent of Diane in the midst of her own worries. It
surprised me really; didn't seem quite like the kind of thing
I'd have expected of her.'

'Don't you like her, darling?' Alison asked curiously.

Michael lifted her hand and idly dropped a kiss into the
soft palm.

'I don't think "like" is the right word for Diane. She's a
strange woman; fascinating in a way. I doubt if either of us
really knows what she's like – under the surface, I mean.'

Alison felt a moment of pure feminine jealousy.

'You think she's attractive then?'

'Oh, immensely!' Michael said openly and honestly –
reassuringly. 'Whatever "oomph" is, she has bags of it! But
there's something else about Diane. I think she's highly

intelligent and yet unbalanced at the same time. A dangerous cocktail I'd say!'

'I'm jealous!' Alison said. Michael laughed and turned her round so that he could kiss her.

'You needn't be, my darling. I love you and only you, now, always, into eternity. Dear, darling, funny, unsophisticated, adorable, lovable Alison Craig.'

She pulled away from him laughing.

'I'd far rather you thought me a "dangerous cocktail"!' she said.

'And so you are, but a different one. No "hooch" about you. You don't frighten me, my darling. I drink you down in one gulp!'

'Silly!' Alison cried happily. 'Oh, Michael, I do love you so much. I wish we could be married tomorrow!'

'Or now!' Michael said huskily, reaching for her lips once again.

Nine

'Of course I understand your reluctance to discuss family matters with me, a complete stranger, Mrs Craig. But you mustn't look on me as you might an ordinary person. I'm really a nurse. And I do so want to help.'

Mrs Craig was tempted to talk, in spite of her first dislike of the rather smart young woman who had brought her some pills from Dr McFaddon. She seemed sympathetic and she badly needed someone to talk to. Alison had gone out again, leaving her alone for the second time that day. Self-pity overcame her reserve.

'I suppose you approve? You think my daughter has made a good choice?'

'On the contrary!' Diane pulled up a chair and sat down. She resisted the temptation to smoke. 'You see, I know Michael Boyce very well. . .too well, you might say. I thought it only fair to warn you, Mrs Craig, for your daughter's sake.'

The older woman sat up suddenly alert and eager.

'Warn me? About what?'

'Well, Alison has been so kind to me, I'd like to do her a good turn. I tried to talk to her this morning but she wouldn't listen to me. You're the only person whose opinion she really values.'

Mrs Craig digested this happily. At least it showed Alison hadn't lost all love for her mother.

'What is it you want to warn me about? You know something to this young man's discredit?'

Diane hesitated. She must go carefully. It could get back to Michael through Alison and then she would have queered her own pitch badly.

'No! I'm not going to be made to tell tales. I'm sorry, Mrs Craig, but it wouldn't be . . . well, right, would it? With me a nurse and Michael Boyce a doctor.'

'Then you *do* know something? Is he married?'

Mrs Craig's eagerness to hear ill of Michael made it so easy, so stupidly easy, that Diane nearly laughed.

'Oh, no, nothing so respectable as that. I really can't say more, Mrs Craig. Besides, it *might* not be true. You know how people gossip and it's nearly always exaggerated. When they talk about men leaving a woman's flat at midnight, if you really find out the facts, it's probably a respectable nine o'clock. No, really, I won't be responsible for passing on evil gossip. It's just that I don't want Alison hurt. She struck me as being so inexperienced and trusting. Of course, she thinks she's madly in love. And he's very handsome. Very charming, too. No wonder her head is turned.'

'And no truer word was spoken!' Mrs Craig said violently. 'She's gone clean off her head if you ask me. I told her he was no good, but she just can't see it. Won't see it.'

'Naturally. She thinks she's in love and she'll champion him to the last. You'll just have to be strong for both of your sakes, Mrs Craig.'

'Me? What can *I* do, lying here alone and ill?'

Diane patted her hand sympathetically.

'It can't be easy for you. Yet in a way maybe the fact that you are alone and, as you say, ill could sway Alison where reason won't move her. I'm sure she loves you deeply, Mrs Craig. If it came to a choice between you and Michael Boyce I think she would choose to stay with you.'

Mrs Craig's eyes opened wider.

'You do? Did she say that?'

'No, of course not. We really didn't go into the question of the future at all. You see, I've no influence with Alison. We're really only strangers still. But I'd like to help her.'

'Why can't you just say what you know about him?'

Diane shook her head.

'Surely you must realize I couldn't do that. For one thing

I've no proof. For another, Alison wouldn't listen to me, and lastly, he could see I lost my job. I'm alone in the world, Mrs Craig, like you, and I have to support myself. If word of this ever reached Dr Boyce's ears, or Dr McFaddon's, how long do you think I'd keep my job? No, I'm trusting you implicitly to keep me out of this. You must promise me.'

'Of course, of course!' Mrs Craig said. 'All the same, what can I do without proof?'

'You can't really do anything!' Diane said smoothly. 'It's what you don't do that will count, Mrs Craig. No doubt they are both hoping that in time Michael Boyce's charm will win you over to an approval of their engagement. You just mustn't be hoodwinked the way poor Alison is. You must be strong for both of you and, in the end, it will mean open war. Michael will be forced to give Alison an ultimatum – you or him.'

'But suppose she is so under his spell she chooses to run off with him?'

'I don't believe she will. I believe you are more important to Alison than anyone in the world.'

They were words Mrs Craig wanted to hear more than anything. Eagerly she accepted them and Diane, too.

'I'm going to get you a cup of tea. It seems so awful you lying here all alone with no one to care for you,' Diane said sympathetically.

Down in the kitchen she waited for the kettle to boil and smiled contentedly. It was all so easy. Of course, when it came to the point, Alison might choose Michael. But not for long. A few more carefully laid plans and Alison would come running.

She took up the tea-tray and Mrs Craig welcomed her back with open arms.

'How kind you are, dear. It's so nice to think I have an ally. I love Alison dearly and I want her happiness more than anything in the world. If I really thought this man was Mr Right, I'd let her marry him with my blessing. But I knew in my bones he wasn't. I just knew it. Now you've confirmed it.'

90

'Ssh!' Diane said soothingly. 'Don't forget that I must not become involved in this. I'll lose my job. You mustn't let your daughter dream we've had this kind of discussion. If she believed we were trying together to break up her association with Michael she might walk out here and now. You wouldn't want that!'

'No, indeed not!' Mrs Craig admitted. 'Don't worry, my dear. I won't involve you. I think you are wise in your handling of this. It won't be what I do, but what I don't do!'

'Yes,' said Diane, pouring out another cup of tea. 'Yes, that's right!'

'Michael, three months, and Mother still refuses to see you. I can't stand much more of it. She just lies in bed, refusing to move, to come downstairs. When I try to talk to her about you, she pretends she can't hear me. Michael, what are we going to do?'

They were in the sitting-room, talking in whispers like guilty conspirators. Michael was beginning to *feel* like a guilty conspirator. If Mrs Craig had been anyone but Alison's mother, he would have called her a stubborn old witch! The situation was really quite impossible. He couldn't just barge into the old lady's bedroom and demand to be heard. Dr McFaddon and Diane had both tried to talk her into reason, but both had failed. Meanwhile his poor darling Alison was distraught with nervous worry and strain.

'It isn't even as if she were behaving hysterically,' Alison said. 'That first day it was just a long tirade against you. Since then she has been quite calm, quite quiet. I can't argue or discuss you with her. If I mention your name, she says, "I won't discuss that man with you, Alison!" and she won't.'

Michael frowned.

'I know! Diane said yesterday that it was hopeless. Your mother has seen her five times and I gather does discuss the situation with her, but only to say that she will never give her consent to our marriage. Diane can't do a thing.'

Alison shivered. During those first few wonderful days, when she and Michael had discovered their love for each other, it had seemed only a matter of time before Mrs Craig, too, would be as happy as they were. She had been filled with hope and happiness. Now her mother had managed to cast a terrible, inescapable shadow over their love. Of course, she was of age when she could marry Michael without her mother's blessing. But she wouldn't do it. And Michael, bless him, had never once suggested it. He'd been so wonderfully patient, wonderfully understanding. Every day her love for him had grown deeper and now she had reached the point where she felt the situation was horribly unfair to him.

'Michael, I've been thinking. Suppose we were to announce our engagement and fix a date for our wedding?'

Michael swung round to face her, his eyes shining, his face aglow with happiness. He caught her hands in his own and held them tightly.

'Oh, *darling*! If you knew how I've longed to hear you say that. I couldn't ask you, but I've wanted desperately for you to reach the conclusion that this is the only way.'

Alison bit her lip, her eyes downcast.

'Michael, I meant . . . well, just to see if it would make any difference.'

She was appalled by the sudden fear and sadness that swept away the happiness in his face. She knew that he had jumped to the conclusion she was willing to marry him without her mother's approval, when really she had meant only to galvanize her mother into at least discussing Michael.

'Oh, darling! Don't look like that. I love you so very much – you do believe it, don't you? You know I love you better than anyone in the world? I want to be married just as much as you do!'

Michael withdrew his hands, hurt and so disappointed that for a moment, patience, tact were gone.

'Your mother's feelings mean more than mine, or your need for me.'

Alison turned pale. She wasn't angry. He was, in a way, justified in his accusation. Not that her mother did mean more – no one in the world meant more to her than Michael. But she couldn't, *couldn't* cause a permanent rift between herself and her mother. Michael could not ask her to do that.

Suddenly Michael pulled her into his arms and began to kiss her. There was no tenderness in his kisses, no gentleness, only a harsh, passionate desire.

Automatically, her body responded and she knew deep within her that here was something she and Michael could not fight against much longer. It wasn't fair to him to keep on with these meetings, this hopelessly frustrating climb to a pinnacle they must not reach. No wonder he had lost patience. It was a strain on her, too. She wanted to belong to him completely, absolutely.

'Michael, if you want me, I—'

He pushed her away with a painful laugh.

'Want you? My God, Alison, I think you believe I am made of stone. It isn't that I couldn't wait for you in ordinary circumstances. If we were engaged, a date fixed for our wedding, I'd wait a year, longer. At least I could be sure you would be mine in the end.'

'But, Michael, how can you doubt that?'

Michael looked at her, staring deep into her eyes. 'Don't you see that your mother is winning this battle? How do I know that in the end you aren't going to capitulate and throw me over?'

She stared back at him, the colour drained from her cheeks, her heart beating wildly.

'But I wouldn't, I *wouldn't*!' she cried.

Michael never took his eyes from her.

'You say that now. But how long can we go on like this? Your mother obviously can afford the time to wait it out. We can't. We're young and we need each other now, not tomorrow, not in five years' time.'

Alison bit her lip.

'I know, but I'm not asking you to wait any longer, Michael. If you want me, then I'll be yours, all yours, now.'

For a moment temptation caught at him. He'd lain awake so many nights, dreaming of the moment when Alison would belong to him; when he could teach her all the delights of physical love, bring her to a new glory, a new wonder. Desire for her tormented his dreams, his waking thoughts. These hours alone with her had become a kind of torture. Now she was offering him release.

But he wouldn't take it . . . he couldn't. She was offering herself to him because of his need for her, not because of hers for him. And even if such a thing could bring her happiness, and knowing her he doubted it, what a transitory happiness it would be! Later, she would be sorry – they would both be sorry. It would turn the innocence and beauty to a sordid false gold of delight. It would reduce love to physical desire and make a sham of their wedding night, their honeymoon.

'No, darling, *no!*' His voice was gentle now. 'Don't you see how it would solve nothing? After a little while, it wouldn't be enough. We'd want more time to be together; we'd hate the deceit. No, that isn't what I want from you, Alison, nor, I know, what you want from me.'

She was crying now, quietly and hopelessly. He was right; Michael nearly always was right. She wouldn't have wanted it this way. She wanted to be his wife, not some girl he desired in secret.

Gently, he took his own handkerchief and wiped the tears that rolled down her cheeks.

'It's all right, sweetheart! It will be all right!' He spoke the words without hope for he could see no immediate solution. Alison heard them but was not comforted. Michael would wait – but for what? It couldn't go on like this. It wasn't fair to anyone, least of all to the man who had just now proved the depth of his love for her.

She drew a long, shuddering breath.

'We'll get married, Michael, despite Mother. Maybe once it is done she'll give in!'

He caught her shoulders and she felt his fingers digging into the soft flesh.

'Don't say that unless you really mean it, Alison. Do you understand? You must realize what you are saying.'

94

'I do, I do!' Alison replied. She had made her choice and she couldn't go back on it. She must not.

'And you'll go through with it?'

'Yes!'

For a long moment, Michael was silent. Had he the right to encourage her in this step? To come between a mother and daughter? Would he regret it? Did Alison know how hard it was going to be for her?

'Michael, I love you!'

Her cry was like an answer to him. He did not doubt her love and his own was a deep-rooted conviction in his heart. Since they felt this way, it must be right for them to marry, regardless of Mrs Craig.

'Then it must be soon!' Michael spoke aloud. 'We must be married soon. No long engagement, no weakening, Alison. Your mother must know you mean to go through with it.'

Alison felt a cold shiver of fear. To strengthen her resolve she clung to Michael, trying to draw strength from him. But she was only momentarily reassured. Once he had driven away, leaving her alone in the house with her mother, she felt that fear return. How could she break the news? What would Mrs Craig say – do?

'I mustn't be afraid!' Alison told herself sharply, walking up the stairs towards her mother's room. 'I've given Michael my promise. A month from today.'

Resolutely, she knocked on her mother's door and went in.

'Diane, you've got to help us!'

Michael's voice was urgent and desperate. Diane went across to the cocktail cabinet and poured him a drink. She showed no sign of her inner feelings. It was obvious from Michael's impulsive unannounced arrival here at her flat, that something had happened. Could it be that dear little Alison had finally 'gone back to mother'? Had she, Diane, and Mrs Craig won?

She handed Michael his drink and sat opposite him, cool, beautifully turned out as usual. But he didn't notice her, and

95

the thought brought a swift shaft of anger which never reached her face. She smiled gently.

'But of course, you know I'll do anything I can, Michael.'

'Yes! You've been a brick, Diane. Now it's all coming to a head. I've just left Alison at her home. She's going to tell Mrs Craig that we're getting married in a month's time.'

Jolted out of her self-control, Diane gasped.

'A month? Married?'

Fear caught at her heart and, close behind it, a grim determination that she would not lose – not now, not after so long. And how long these last three months had been. A long, terrible wait for Michael to turn to her. But he would, he *must*. To make him her own had become the one governing determining factor in her life. Everything else had ceased to matter. She had to have him, to own him, to possess him. She was, herself, like a woman possessed.

'Yes! But I'm afraid, Diane – afraid Alison might not be strong enough to go through with it. You've got to help her, make her realize it's the right thing.'

'I see!'

She looked down at her long pointed red nails and, seeming to study them, her mind raced onwards. Alison wasn't yet beyond hope. She could be weakened; it could still be prevented, provided Mrs Craig kept her head.

I'll have to see her! she thought quickly. Bolster her up. Last time she was beginning to weaken. Stupid woman! As if it mattered that Alison showed no love for her. She must put up with that if she wants her back in the end. How many times do I have to tell her that!

'You're quite sure it . . . well, that it is the right thing?'

'Sure? Of course I'm sure, Diane. Don't tell me you think a girl like Alison should spend the rest of her life tied to that old woman's apron strings?'

'No, no of course not!' Diane agreed soothingly. (How handsome Michael was when he was angry, how much more attractive even than when he smiled!) 'I just wondered if it was the right thing to do to hurry this marriage on. Wouldn't it be safer to be patient a while longer?'

'To what purpose? Nothing will change. Her mother's mind is made up. Waiting won't help, and Diane, I can't wait much longer. Oh, I suppose that sounds crazy and it isn't true. But it's affecting my work.'

'Poor old boy!' She moved across and laid a cool hand on his shoulder. 'I do understand. Desire can play the devil, can't it?'

Her nearness, her perfume, her soft voice, were all around him. He realized suddenly that this wasn't just Diane Fellows, nurse, friend. This was a woman, soft, supple, feminine, like Alison, yet not Alison.

'How tired I am!' The words fell from his lips as he leant his head against the back of the chair and closed his eyes. 'What a muddle it all is. If I could only be sure she meant to go through with it.'

Diane sat on the arm of the chair and resisted the temptation to touch him.

'I can't understand why she has taken so long to reach this conclusion,' she said in feigned surprise. 'After all, if she feels the same way about you as you feel about her, she must be pretty frustrated by now, too.'

Michael sighed.

'Oh, it's different. Alison is so completely innocent. She doesn't understand – how could she, poor darling?'

'But I understand!' Diane said quietly. 'I, too, have known the heights of physical love. Really, we're two of a kind, aren't we? Both tormented and frustrated by a need for someone we can't have?'

The subtle suggestion did not escape him. He knew then that this woman wanted him. Had it not been for Alison – but Alison existed, pure, sweet, believing in him. He couldn't do anything to sully that faith, that trust.

She read the momentary temptation in his face, saw his eyes recognizing her as a woman, a desirable woman, and her heart leapt.

She reached out her hand and gently pushed the lock of dark hair off his forehead.

'Don't do that!' he said sharply.

97

She gave a long husky laugh.

'Your nerves are in pieces, Michael. Relax! Lie back and have a sleep if you like. If you go on like this you'll be cracking up yourself!'

He sighed, remembering now that Diane, too, had her problems.

'Things any better for you?' he asked.

'No!' It was a bald statement of fact. He felt sorry for her. It seemed such a terrible waste that a woman like Diane, as attractive as Diane, should spend her life alone, longing for someone who didn't give a row of pins for her.

'Funny!' he mused aloud. 'I should have thought any man would have had a job to resist you, Diane.'

'Do you, Michael? Yet you don't see me as irresistible. You are blinded by your love for Alison – blind to my so-called charms!'

Michael laughed.

'No! I'm still capable of seeing how damned attractive you are, my girl. Dangerously so. I should have thought this chap you're in love with must also have eyes to see.'

'Maybe!' Diane said softly. 'But he isn't in love with me. Still, it's nice to know one man finds me attractive.'

'I've got to go!' Michael said suddenly. 'If I don't, you'll be giving me ideas you'd regret.'

'Maybe I wouldn't regret them!'

No, maybe not! Michael thought. But he would. What a strange woman Diane was. In some curious way, her attitude to life was more that of a man, and yet there never existed a more feminine woman. A dangerous combination . . . it wasn't every day a woman like Diane offered herself without obligations or a cry for love, and yet was so essentially feminine, desirable. He was well aware that women had a basic need of love, physical love, just the same as men.

'Diane, I *must* go. I've a mountain of work. McFaddon will be giving me the sack if I don't pull my socks up.'

She knew she'd lost. Momentarily, anger and frustration twisted her mouth into a hard line. But she quickly controlled herself. No time now for recriminations, no place for appeals. They wouldn't touch Michael in his present mood of self-denial for Alison's sake. But the time would come . . . the time when Alison had chucked him over and he needed someone else. . . .

'See you soon!' she said lightly, showing him to the door. 'Any time at all you want to "get away from it all" you can always come here.'

'You're a good sport, Diane, and a good friend!' Michael said. 'I'll be back!'

'Yes, I'll see to that!' Diane thought as she closed the door behind him and hurried up to her room to change her clothes.

Ten

Mrs Craig gave her daughter a quick look which held in it fear, anxiety and concern. Alison had lost weight these last weeks and there were dark shadows beneath her eyes. She didn't look at all well.

It's that beast of a man! she told herself sharply. He is responsible for this, not I.

But she wasn't altogether happy. Just for an instant, she began to doubt if Diane Fellows' advice was right after all. She loved Alison dearly and it was only for her good that she had stuck out against her engagement to Dr Boyce. Had she liked him and believed him to be a good man and right for Alison, she would have given way weeks ago. She couldn't bear to see Alison's distraught, unhappy eyes looking at her so pleadingly – yet she *must* remain firm. It was a classic example of being cruel to be kind.

'Mother!'

'Yes, dear?'

'Michael and I are getting married next month!'

It was out, said and she must not withdraw it. Alison watched her mother's face, seeing the kindness and sympathy drain away to be replaced by anger and fear.

'Over my dead body!' Mrs Craig said bluntly and cruelly. 'I'll never give my consent, Alison. If you marry that man I'll never speak to you again.'

'You don't really mean that – you *can't*!' Alison cried.

'I do mean it!' Mrs Craig flung back at her. 'It is for *your* sake, Alison, not mine.'

Alison's cheeks were flushed now where a moment before they had been pale.

'How can you say that, Mother? What gives you the right to judge Michael? You haven't even spoken to him. What have you got against him?'

Many a time these same questions had remained unanswered. All too often, Mrs Craig had replied, 'I won't discuss it!' But now, surprisingly, she did.

'Very well, since you insist, I'll tell you, Alison. I happen to know that he's immoral. No, don't interrupt me. Of course you won't want to believe this – you're far too much under his influence. But you asked me why I object and I'm telling you. He's *no good.*'

'Prove it!' Alison cried. 'You haven't seen anybody but myself and Dr McFaddon and Diane Fellows for weeks. Who can have been gossiping about Michael to you? You're making it up!'

Mrs Craig's lips tightened.

'I am not in the habit of lying, Alison, and I give you my word of honour that I am not fabricating this story. I have heard on reliable authority that this doctor of yours is in the habit of staying late at night in a young woman patient's flat. He visits her frequently, and all the time he goes on seeing you and no doubt telling you you are the only girl in the world!'

Alison sat down in the basket chair, the strength gone from her limbs. Of course, she didn't believe a word of it, but who could have been saying such things about Michael? Strangely, she believed her mother when she said she had not made this story up. There was a ring of truth in her voice and besides, no one would care to say such libellous things unless they believed them true.

'You'd have to give me proof, Mother, before I'd believe it.'

Mrs Craig looked at her daughter hopefully.

'And if I could get proof, you'd give him up?'

'Certainly!' Alison said, knowing that it *couldn't* be true. Michael wasn't like that; she'd trust him to the end of the world.

'Very well then!' Mrs Craig cried triumphantly. 'In the

101

meanwhile I think it would be only fair to postpone the announcement of this wedding. I'll get your proof for you.'

'You seem very sure you can,' Alison said with a shiver. 'All right, Mother, I'll wait till the weekend. After that, I shall announce our wedding in the local paper.'

'You won't!' Mrs Craig said. 'I *know* you won't!'

She never doubted she would obtain the proof. Alison must believe Diane Fellows. She'd often said what a good friend she had become, both to her and Michael and to her mother. And Diane would surely offer proof. Diane must be made to come round immediately.

I'll wait until Alison is at work tomorrow, and phone Diane, she thought.

But there was no need. Not long after Monday morning surgery had finished Diane Fellows let herself in by the back door and went up to Mrs Craig's room.

Diane smiled grimly.

'So you've heard the news!'

'Yes! It's got to be stopped, Diane, at all costs. And there's only one way to do it. Alison has given me her word that if I can prove what you say about Dr Boyce, she'll give him up.'

Diane knew a moment's swift fear. Had Mrs Craig blurted out the lies she had fabricated about Michael's affair with a woman patient?

'You didn't tell Alison I—'

'No, no, my dear! I promised you I wouldn't mention your name. I just said I knew what he'd been up to and that I could prove it. Of course, we haven't legal proof, but I'm sure Alison would take your word.'

Silly fool! Diane thought harshly. She dared not be dragged in. Apart from anything else, to say such things was slander. Of all the silly things to have done; but it was too late now. Somehow, she must think up a way out of this. Something near enough to fact to be convincing. But what? As far as she knew, Michael led a blameless life!

'You can – you *will* help?' Mrs Craig was asking anxiously.

'Of course! The thing is, how to convince Alison. I'm

102

afraid she's far too much in love to take my word. After all, as you say, I can't give legal proof. And without it, we dare not mention this other woman's name.'

Mrs Craig looked even more anxious.

'But surely, if you *know*. . .you said you'd seen him leaving her flat on a number of occasions – in broad daylight, too!'

'Yes, yes! But we don't want a case of slander against us, do we? And we haven't time to put a private detective on to him. If Alison warns him what is in the wind, he'll take good care not to be seen again.'

'Then what can we do? Alison says she's going to announce her wedding at the weekend unless she has proof. We must save her from herself.'

Diane smiled a grim, humourless smile which never touched her eyes.

'There is a way!' she said thoughtfully. 'But it won't be easy.'

'Tell me!' the old lady begged.

'Well, as you know, I'd do anything to help Alison, and you. I've grown so fond of you both and you've been so good to me. It would mean my losing Alison's friendship – for a while, anyway, but I'm willing, if you think it will help.'

'But what? What do you mean?' Mrs Craig asked.

'Simply that I tell her *I* am the other woman – the one Michael comes to see.'

'*You?*' Mrs Craig was deeply shocked.

'Of course, I don't mean I am!' Diane said quickly, reassuringly. 'But I'm willing to say I am, for your sake and for mine. I know it's not quite the truth, but a white lie is a small price to pay for Alison's happiness, isn't it?'

'But your reputation, your job. . .' Mrs Craig stuttered. 'If Dr Boyce heard he'd be bound to sack you.'

'Would he? After all, he knows who the woman really is. He might do anything to prevent her name coming out. I could promise not to reveal it provided he let me keep my job and provided he gave up Alison.'

While the older woman pondered this scheme, Diane's

103

mind raced forward. Mrs Craig would have to help, pretend to be horrified, scandalized, unwilling to see her any more. When Alison charged her with the truth of what she said, she, Diane, would simply deny it. 'Naturally, Alison, your mother will say anything to keep you from marrying Michael. Of course, I'm shocked that she should have picked on me as a scapegoat, but I suppose I'm the only person she could think of. It shows how desperate she is not to lose you.' Yes, it would be easy to tell Alison it was all her mother's fabrication. Michael, too, if it came to his ears. A good idea if it did. Michael would be furious at any slur on his reputation; it would turn him further against Mrs Craig and he'd force Alison into a choice between them.

It might be dangerous for her, but then who would take the word of a hysterical, biased, neurotic old woman?

'Well?'

Mrs Craig looked down at her hands, nervously pleating the edge of the sheet.

'It hardly seems fair to you . . .' she began weakly. But it wasn't many minutes before Diane convinced her no harm would be done. There was no real risk and everything to be gained.

'Very well! You'll come this evening and "confess" to Alison?'

'No, of course I can't do that. It wouldn't ring true. As if I would stay in person to face the music. No, no, you'll have to tell her that you'd heard from me about this other woman; that when you questioned me today, you discovered that it was really me all the time. Naturally, you'll be appalled and never want to see me again.'

'You mean, I shan't see you again?'

'Oh, but of course!' Diane said soothingly. 'But, naturally, I won't come when Alison is about. But not for a week or two.'

Mrs Craig looked unhappy.

'I don't really like this,' she said petulantly. 'It seems so involved and I hate lying. If Alison found out . . .'

Yes, thought Diane suddenly. There is a risk it will turn

104

Alison against her mother and into Michael's arms. But if that happened, then there were other measures. She'd think of something to keep them apart. Diane Fellows didn't give in so easily when she wanted something as passionately as she wanted Michael Boyce. She'd do anything short of murder to get him. He had become an obsession in her life. Nothing else mattered now. With a fanatic's single-mindedness, she had set herself the task of obtaining what she wanted. Nothing and no one would stop her.

'Remember we *must* go through with this for your daughter's sake. Just remind yourself how bitterly unhappy she would be, a decent, well-brought-up girl like Alison, to learn *after* her marriage that her husband was prepared to make love to another woman whilst professing to love her!'

'Yes, yes, that's true. My poor baby; she's going to suffer, but better now than later. All right, Diane, we'll do what you say. When she comes home this evening, I'll tell her.'

Neither woman thought too happily about the plan as the day wore on. Mrs Craig, really a kindly, decent woman at heart, baulked at the necessary lies. Diane, alone in her flat, began to fear that this might be the turning point in Alison's life; that she might turn away from her mother, straight into Michael's waiting arms. She'd have to be very careful what she said when Alison came round to ask her to her face if it was true. Better, perhaps, to *admit* to an affair with Michael. But no, Alison might tackle him and then her own position with Michael would be ruined for always!

Anxiously, she watched the hands of the clock turn. Admit or deny? Best, perhaps, to wait and see how Alison took her mother's news. If she disbelieved it, best deny it. If she was suspicious, then it would be safer to admit to an affair and warn Alison that naturally Michael would deny it. Wait and see. But waiting did not come easily and she paced the floor, to and fro, like an animal in a cage. She was excited and afraid and both emotions stimulated her so that she could not rest.

Quite suddenly her mind jumped with an idea. Somehow

105

she must get Michael here, in the flat. Keep him here. Then if Alison came round she'd find them together.

But how to get Michael? He was on his afternoon rounds. There was six o'clock surgery. If she could persuade him at the end of it to come back with her for a drink – but how, how? Maybe he was meeting Alison! She'd think of a way. She had an hour left to think of a way.

Tired from the day's work, Alison went wearily home. She had barely slept the night before, lying awake, thinking about her mother's absurd accusations against Michael. She did not for a single instant believe them. But she was appalled by the thought that her mother *could* lie on such a serious matter. Maybe someone with a grudge against Michael had written an anonymous letter; maybe Michael had had an affair in the past. Few men of Michael's age had had celibate lives before they fell in love and married. She wouldn't let his past interfere with the present. It was past, gone. But who could have done such a thing? Only someone who knew that she and Michael were in love – someone living locally. And how did they know about Michael's life in England? He'd met her, Alison, almost as soon as he'd arrived in Scotland.

So her mind had twisted in circles and now, after a day at the factory, she felt washed out and exhausted.

She had barely been in the house a minute before her mother called her. Obediently, Alison climbed the stairs and went into Mrs Craig's room.

Her mother's face was flushed and almost excited.

'Well, I have the proof you wanted!' she announced.

'Proof I wanted?' Alison repeated with a hard little laugh. 'It wasn't me who wanted proof, Mother, but you. Well, let's hear it. I can see you can't wait to tell me, though how you've managed to get proof of anything when you've lain here in bed all day, I don't know!'

'Of course, you're sarcastic now, my girl!' Mrs Craig said impatiently. 'I knew you'd be unwilling to face facts. Well, sit down and I'll tell you.'

'All right!' said Alison, wearily sinking into the chair. 'Tell me. Who is she?'

Mrs Craig drew a deep breath.

'Diane Fellows!'

Alison sat up suddenly and completely alert.

'You mean Diane told you about this friend of Michael's?'

'Yes, she told me, and *she is the woman*!'

For a moment Alison was too taken aback to think. Diane . . . but that wasn't possible – it was absurd. As if Michael would have carried on an affair with Diane behind her back! And yet her mother couldn't be making it up. She must know she had only to go round to Diane's flat to hear her deny it.

'Mother, that is a terrible lie!' she said at last. 'I don't believe it and I don't think you realize how awful it is for me to have to hear you say such things. Oh, Mother, don't go on with this. I love Michael, I'm going to marry him. Nothing you can say will stop me, so please, *please* don't go on saying these terrible things.'

She pleaded in vain.

'You gave me your word that if you had proof, you'd call off the wedding.'

'But you haven't given me any proof!' Alison said. 'I can't help it, Mother, but I just don't believe you.'

'It's true, all the same. She stood here in this room and confessed it to me. I don't see why it's so hard to believe. She's attractive and a widow; she lives alone.'

'And she'll confess to me, too?' Alison asked. 'You don't mind my going round to see her, to ask her if it's true?'

'Not in the least!' Mrs Craig retorted uneasily.

For the first time, suspicion caught at Alison's heart. So her mother wasn't lying. But Diane had professed to be her friend. No, Michael, no! she thought. Yet it could be. . .

Suddenly, she remembered the night Diane had rung Michael here, begging him to go round quickly. She'd tried to kill herself because she'd been in love with someone who didn't love her. Michael! The pieces of the jigsaw were falling into place.

107

'No, no, *no!*' she cried aloud. 'I won't . . . I can't believe it.'

Mrs Craig looked at her daughter sympathetically.

'But you are beginning to believe me. Go round and see that woman. Of course, it shocked me terribly. All this while she had pretended to be my friend, had sat here in this room, telling me how fond she was of you. She begged me to stay firm in my refusal to countenance an engagement. When I pressed her for her reasons, she told me this doctor of yours was having an affair with a woman in the town. I'd have told you long ago only you wouldn't listen to anything against him. I believed you'd come to your senses in the end. You can see now why she pressed me to make you give him up; she wants him for herself. And in my view, he ought to marry her.'

'Stop it!' Alison cried, jumping up. 'I won't listen. I won't believe it until both of them admit it to me. I shall ask Michael. He won't lie to me.'

Mrs Craig snorted.

'You expect him to admit it? Of course he won't.'

'I think he would, if it were true!' Alison cried. 'I suppose it might not have occurred to you, Mother, that Diane could be lying? Suppose she is in love with Michael, wants him for herself. What better way to break up the affair between Michael and myself than to spread the rumour he's in love with her?'

Mrs Craig gave a snort of genuine indignation.

'Diane only told me the truth to save you from getting hurt!'

'Rubbish!' Alison said rudely. 'This is a terrible tangle of lies, Mother, and I can assure you that it is all quite useless. Michael isn't like that. I know him. I trust him.'

Mrs Craig lay back against the pillows.

'I didn't expect you to believe me. Ring *him!*'

'Very well, I will!'

Alison felt a moment's shiver of apprehension as she went downstairs to the hall to telephone. She didn't really believe one word of all this, and yet her mother seemed so certain, so sure of herself.

108

She dialled the surgery number with trembling fingers. It was Dr McFaddon who answered.

'Could I please speak to Michael?' Alison asked. 'That is, if he isn't too busy.'

'Surgery's over, my dear!' Dr McFaddon said kindly. 'But I'm afraid Michael isn't here. He went back to Nurse Fellows' flat to fetch something he'd left there or she had borrowed, I'm not sure which. I don't suppose he'll be back here tonight; he's off ,duty this evening. Perhaps you'd get him later at his digs?'

Alison thanked the old doctor and replaced the receiver, feeling the sweat break out on the palms of her hands. No, no! she cried. It can't be true! I still won't believe it!

What should she do now? Phone Diane's flat? But then what could she say when Diane answered. She could ring Michael at his digs later. But she couldn't wait. If it were all true and not just some horrible nightmare from which she would presently awake, she must *know* now.

I'll go round there! she thought. I'll face both of them – together!

Without telling her mother, she flung on her coat and ran out of the house. She had to wait on the corner nearly five minutes for a bus and then it was crowded. But she stood for the short journey into the west side of town where Diane's flat was situated.

Outside the door of Diane's flat, Alison paused. Wild impulse had driven her here but now she was no longer sure she really wanted to know the truth. Would it not be better to go on living in a dream, believing, loving? Life would be so empty and cold and unbearable without Michael's love.

She shook the hair from her forehead and tossed back her head, her eyes brilliant and determined. No, that would mean living in a world of deceit. Such ways were not for her.

She leaned forward and rang the bell.

'Why, Alison, what a pleasant surprise!'

Alison gave Diane a long, slow look from angry eyes. She ignored the polite welcome.

'Is Michael here?'

'Yes! Did you want to see him? Come right up! He was just going.'

A little shaken by Diane's casualness, Alison followed the older girl upstairs. Diane preceded her into the sitting-room where Michael stood, his back to the electric fire, sipping a drink. His face lit up as he caught sight of Alison and he moved forward with a cry of welcome.

'Darling, how lovely!' He paused as she stepped backwards, avoiding his embrace. Puzzled, he wondered first it she were shy in Diane's presence, but then, seeing her windswept hair and flushed cheeks, he began to sense something more was causing her restraint.

'Anything wrong, darling?' he asked.

'If it's anything private, I can easily make myself scarce!' Diane broke in smoothly.

Alison shot her a quick look.

'No, stay, Diane! I think you should hear what my mother has been saying. She . . .' Alison looked back at Michael, staring into his dark eyes, seeing only concern, surprise in their questioning gaze.

'Well?' he prompted her.

'She says . . . she told me that Diane had been to see her today and that you, Diane, had told her you and Michael had been having an affair – that you were in love.'

Michael's laugh was like a wonderful soothing balm on an open wound. Hearing it, feeling his arms go round her, Alison knew that she had had no need to be afraid, to suspect.

'My darling, you didn't believe her! Oh, Alison!'

Diane watched them, her eyes suddenly hard and furious. So it hadn't worked. And Michael had laughed. *Laughed!* As if an affair with her, Diane, was the last thing in the world he would ever contemplate.

You'll pay for this! she thought with a quick angry venom. Michael had turned from Alison to look at her and she quickly changed her expression to one of hurt indignation.

'Diane, did you hear that? We're supposed to be having an affair! Really, Alison, your mother ought to be more

110

careful. Such accusations amount to slander, you know.'

Alison sank down into the nearest chair.

'I know!' she said. 'But, Michael, she seemed so completely convinced she was right. What I don't understand is that if she had made it all up, been bluffing, then why didn't she object when I said I'd confront you both with the truth?'

'She has probably convinced herself it is true!' Michael said, sitting on the arm of the chair and running a hand through Alison's hair. 'Sweetheart, surely you trust me?'

She looked up at him, shame now in her eyes.

'Yes, I do! But I had to come and ask you first.'

'Diane, what happened at Mrs Craig's this afternoon? Was she behaving very oddly? I mean, did you have any idea this was at the back of her mind?'

Diane hesitated. She must go carefully now.

'Well, things were a bit strained. She kept hurling accusations at Michael, saying nonsensical things about his past. I wasn't really paying a lot of attention, but she did turn on me, too. She said I was no better than you; but all the medical profession were bad. Everyone knew what medical students and nurses got up to and for all she knew, you and I . . . oh, but it's too silly, Michael. I never pay any attention when she flies off the handle like that. I always think it's best to let patients get it off their chests.'

Alison looked at Diane curiously.

'Mother said you'd *told* her you were having an affair!'

'Well, I don't intend any disrespect to your mother, Alison, but quite honestly I agree with Michael. You ought to restrain her or else one day she will be in for a libel action.'

Quite suddenly Alison felt sick. It was so horrid to hear her darling mother spoken of in such terms.

'Please, Michael, will you take me home?' she asked quietly.

'Of course, darling. And when we get there, I'm going in to see that mother of yours. Now don't argue with me, I've made up my mind. I shan't be unkind – just firm. It's high

111

time she realized that such goings-on are a waste of her time. I'm not going to have you bullied and upset and turned into a nervous wreck any longer. I'm going to tell her, Alison, that we're going to be married a month from today.'

Eleven

So confident was Mrs Craig of victory that when she heard the front door open she called down to Alison eagerly:
'Is that you, dear? Come up quickly!'

She couldn't wait another minute to hear that Alison had finally made the break with Michael. That Diane would have convinced her that Michael was no good, she was happily certain.

Hearing two sets of footsteps on the stairs, her face contorted into a puzzled frown. Had Diane come back with Alison? When the bedroom door opened and Michael Boyce came in, Mrs Craig turned a ghastly white from genuine shock.

'Mother, Michael wants to tell you something!'

Alison made no move to her mother's bedside but stood beside Michael, her mouth trembling but determined. She wouldn't weaken. Never again would she let her mother cast suspicion on the man she loved.

'How dare you!' Mrs Craig burst out. 'How dare you come here like this.'

'I have come to tell you something, Mrs Craig. Since you refuse to accept that Alison and I want to be married, I have been forced to come here and tell you in person. Alison has agreed to marry me and the wedding will be in a month's time. We would both like you to be present at the wedding and Alison, naturally, would like to be married from her own home. However, if you refuse this, Alison will be married from a hotel.'

Mrs Craig looked from Michael's stern face to Alison's white one.

113

'You're not going to do this, Alison? You know he's immoral and worthless and evil. *I won't let you!*'

'You can't stop me, Mother. And please don't go on saying things about Michael which aren't true.'

'So you haven't seen Diane Fellows!' Mrs Craig cried. 'She'll tell you the truth. You ask her about this man—'

'Stop it, Mother! Michael and I have just come from Diane's flat. Of course she never admitted to any of the vile accusations you have made about her or Michael.'

Mrs Craig was momentarily confused. What had gone wrong? Diane had promised to admit everything. Had she been afraid to do so at the last minute?

She felt suddenly old and tired and terribly alone. Her confusion and distress showed all too plainly in her face and impulsively Alison ran across to the bed and, kneeling beside it, took her mother's hand in her own two warm ones.

'Mummy, don't go on with this fight. It won't do any good. You know I can't bear to go on quarrelling with you like this. I love you far too much. Let's make a fresh start and all three of us be friends – please, Mummy!'

For a moment Mrs Craig was tempted. Genuinely devoted to Alison, the feud had upset her as much, if not more, than it had Alison. She longed to be on good terms with Alison again, to hear love and sympathy and affection in her voice instead of anger and irritation. But to give way now was weakness. For Alison's sake she must fight against her weak longing to give in and go on trying to protect her from herself, from this man who was so unworthy to be her husband.

She drew her hand away sharply and her mouth tightened.

'I'll never give my consent!' She spoke the words slowly and distinctly. 'Never, as long as I live!'

Michael stood looking down at her with a puzzled frown. What reason could this woman have to hate him so much? There was more here than just jealousy. Surely she couldn't really believe all those impossible accusations she had made about him and Diane Fellows? Was she out of her mind?

Alison stood up and Michael was shocked to see the tears

114

pouring down her cheeks. She was crying silently and seemed unaware of the fact as she moved to Michael's side and clasped his hand.

'Come on, Michael,' she said, and without a backward glance at the woman in the bed, she pulled him from the room.

Downstairs in the living-room she clung to him with a desperation that frightened him. He felt her need for assurance that she had made the right choice, but for once his own feeling of certainty had deserted him. It was something odd in Mrs Craig's manner; something he had felt or sensed which he could not explain but which had made him feel she wasn't play-acting now.

'Darling, if you'd rather postpone . . .' he began, but now it was Alison who was strong.

'No, Michael. It will serve no purpose. Mother has set her heart against you and that's all there is to it. Maybe after it's all over she'll give in. She *must*. She can't live here alone.'

'No!' Michael agreed. For even if she were not the invalid she liked to make out, Mrs Craig could still not be expected to live alone. She must make her home with them. But what kind of a home would it be where he and Alison's mother were not on speaking terms?

He kissed her suddenly and passionately, trying to forget his own apprehensions in the sweet excitement of her lips. Feeling her tremble beneath his touch, he felt a desperate responsibility for her. His coming into her life had had such a marked impact on all that was known and familiar to her. Deliberately, he had opened her eyes to a new life, to love, to a cold analysis of her mother and the choice of roads which lay before her. Tonight had been the turning point and Alison had chosen to go his way, with him, trusting and believing in him. By doing so, it meant she was turning her back on the person nearest and hitherto dearest to her. Had he the right to let her do this for him? Surely Mrs Craig *must* weaken. She had no one else but Alison in the world. How had she held out so long? And what real reason did she have to hate him so much? Her whole behaviour was that of a woman defending her young, and yet in her heart she must *know* the evil things she said were, to put it kindly, pure imagination.

'Darling!' He raised her face so that he could look into her eyes. 'You do trust me, don't you?'

'You know I do!' Alison cried without hesitation.

'You'll never let anything anyone says come between us?'

'Of course not!' Alison promised, feeling mean now for ever having doubted Michael. Here in his arms, her suspicions seemed despicable. She wasn't even going to ask him what he was doing this evening in Diane's flat.

But as if in direct telepathic understanding of her thoughts, Michael said:

'I wonder if your mother heard any gossip about Diane? I have had to go to her flat once or twice and maybe my name has been linked with hers. Perhaps she does have a man friend there occasionally and someone seeing me there has put two and two together and made five.'

'You go often?' Alison asked curiously.

Michael sat down in the armchair and pulled her down on to his lap.

'No, sweetheart. Three times in all to be exact. Once, soon after I'd first met you, I went there for a drink. Then there was the time she had that accident – and tonight. She rang through to say she'd left the surgery with my stethoscope, so I dropped by to pick it up on my way home and stayed for a quick drink before coming round to see you. I suppose some scandal-mongering neighbour *might* have been peering from behind lace curtains and recognized my car. I'll have to watch out. A doctor's reputation is pretty important to him.'

'Michael, have you ever been in love before?'

It was a purely feminine question and Michael smiled.

'I thought I was, dozens of times. But I knew they meant nothing the day I fell in love with you. Why, you've armed me even against the charms of a girl like Diane!'

'Then you find her attractive?'

116

Michael laughed again and dropped a quick kiss on her hair.

'I can see with my eyes that she is attractive! But I don't feel it here!' He put his hand over his heart. 'There is no room here for anyone but you, my darling!'

Somehow in that moment Alison felt Michael dedicate himself to her and, in the impulsive kiss she gave him in return, so did she dedicate herself and her future to him.

In the brief and rather unromantic wedding service in the registrar's office three weeks later, she thought back to this moment and knew that the service was only a legal signing of a pledge already given.

Michael did his best to make the day happy for her. He had prevailed on kindly, sympathetic old Dr McFaddon to act as one of the witnesses. Diane had been the second witness. But the ceremony was blighted by the conspicuous absence of Alison's mother.

For Michael's sake Alison had taken immense trouble with her appearance. She wore the beautiful spray of orange blosson and lily of the valley Michael had given her on the lapel of the brand new pale-blue suit, bought for her wedding. She tried her best to feel like a bride. But all the time, she thought of her mother, grim, silent and unwavering. Lying alone in her room. She had cruelly refused even her good wishes on this day. Diane was the only one of the four to appear in good spirits. She looked magnificent in an emerald-green tight-fitting suit with a tiny fur cap hugging her dark head.

Alison looked at her with gratitude. But for her, they might not be having a honeymoon, for Alison could not have borne to go away leaving her mother alone in that empty house. Diane had suggested she stay there the fortnight she and Michael went to England.

'You needn't worry about a thing!' Diane had told them. 'After all I am a nurse and no one could take better care than I do!'

It had astonished both Michael and Alison that Mrs Craig had agreed to having Diane in the house. After all, Diane was supposed to be the other 'immoral partner in crime'; but, as Michael had pointed out, if Mrs Craig had made it all up she'd known all along that Diane was as guiltless as he.

The ceremony in the registrar's office over, Michael and his bride and the two witnesses were to celebrate with a small lunch in Diane's flat. That afternoon they were to start the drive south in Michael's car, stopping somewhere en route for the night. Alison tried desperately to keep her mind on these plans, but somehow her thoughts kept returning to her mother.

It was Michael, understanding and sympathetic as ever, who said after the wedding:

'Would you like to pop home first, sweetheart, and give your mother your flowers?'

She loved him deeply and truly and with immense gratitude at that moment. He was so generous where her mother was concerned. If only Mrs Craig would be as generous, too.

But her mother was not so kind or considerate of her feelings, Alison thought bitterly. This was her wedding day and should be the happiest in her life, but her mother had no thought except for herself.

'No, Michael!' she told her young husband. 'I'd rather stay with you.'

Michael held her tightly in his arms. They had driven back to Diane's flat ahead of the other two and these were their first moments alone since they had become man and wife.

'Mrs Michael Boyce!' he said, smiling tenderly. 'Oh, darling, I find it hard to believe. I wish . . .'

He broke off, but she prompted him quickly.

'What do you wish, Michael?'

'Oh, only that your mother felt differently. I know how you would have liked a white wedding and a reception at home, with your mother happy and co-operative about everything.'

Privately, Alison agreed. She felt that because of her mother the day had been marred for Michael as much as for her, and silently she vowed to make it up to him.

'I think that's Doc's car!' Michael said. 'Kiss me, my dear, darling wife!'

Alison kissed him swiftly, passionately, and he released her only as the door opened and Diane and Dr McFaddon came in.

Diane knew instantly by the self-conscious look on the newly weds' faces that she had interrupted an embrace. Her body felt cold with a suppressed anger and jealousy. But the bright, friendly smile she gave them betrayed none of her inner feelings.

She had been clever enough to know when Michael and Alison announced their forthcoming wedding despite Mrs Craig's refusal of consent, that she had lost the first round. To try to prevent the wedding then was to throw away the game altogether. She must let the wedding take place, aid them in every way possible, become the trusted friend once more. Then . . . then . . .

But it wasn't easy to see Michael so ardently and passionately attracted to his bride. It wasn't easy to have to watch them holding hands, looking into each other's eyes, obviously deeply and tenderly in love. It wasn't easy to play the part of hostess at their wedding lunch, to hear Doc McFaddon toast them and their future, to see them drive away in Michael's car on their honeymoon.

But she carried out her part in the performance without a slip. She was strengthened by her obsessional plans for the day when *she* would be the companion at Michael's side; *she* the bride to share his bed. She never doubted that day would come. The fact that she had first to break up the marriage she had helped this day to take place meant nothing. She could and would do so without a qualm.

'But how?' Mrs Craig asked tearfully when Diane sat by her bed an hour or two afterwards. Always weak, she had become now as emotionally dependent on Diane as once she had been on Alison. It had been easy for Diane Fellows to gain complete domination over her, and Diane had easily forced her to hold out to the last against the wedding.

It hadn't been easy for Mrs Craig to lie there silent and

119

alone, knowing that Alison, her only child, was being married. Had it not been for Diane, she would have given way; it had nearly broken her heart to hold out against Alison's last desperate appeal to her to come to her wedding. And now it was all over; Alison had gone on her honeymoon.

'I have a plan!' Diane said quietly. 'I think it is the only hope, Mrs Craig.'

'But have we the right to break up her marriage, even if it is to the wrong man!' Mrs Craig argued doubtfully. 'After all, the service does say "Those whom God hath joined together, let no man put asunder"!'

'But God hasn't joined them together!' Diane retorted, smoothly. 'They're only married by law. It's hardly a real marriage at all.'

Mrs Craig looked at her companion uncertainly. It was a comfort to think that a registrar's office wedding wasn't really the real thing, and yet, if it were not, it meant that Alison and that man had gone away for a week together and would be living 'in sin'. She was shocked and relieved at once.

'Now listen,' Diane said firmly. 'You've been wonderful so far, Mrs Craig, and I know that one day Alison will thank you for showing such firmness and strength of character. You must go on being strong and determined.'

'Yes, yes, I will,' Mrs Craig agreed. 'But what are we going to do?'

'We're going to prove to Alison that you really are ill!' Diane said. 'Oh, I know Michael Boyce doesn't think so. But I believe you are, Mrs Craig. I've seen plenty of physical suffering as a nurse and I recognize pain in someone's face when I see it. Now, suppose we get a specialist to say you really are ill. Don't you see what this will mean to Alison? She'll realize that Michael Boyce was wrong in his diagnosis; that he deliberately misled her into believing you were pretending illness in order to stop her marrying and having a life of her own. Because that is what she does think, Mrs Craig. I've heard Michael tell her so with my own ears.'

Mrs Craig was crying quietly with self-pity. Everything Diane said was true. Alison used to be so sympathetic and understanding about her attacks until Dr Boyce came on the scene. It was he who had set Alison against her. The sooner he was unmasked the better and then Alison would come home of her own accord.

'Now don't cry!' Diane said, concealing her irritation. 'It will only make you feel bad again. I'm going to write to a specialist I know who deals with nothing else but nervous disorders. I shall tell him all your symptoms and he'll write back and tell me his views. I feel sure he'll agree with me that you need specialist treatment. When we get his report we can send it to Alison, can't we? And then we can begin to get you well again.'

Diane lay awake long into the night, thinking over her plan. It was dangerous. She could fake a reply from the specialist, a hypothetical specialist, of course. But it couldn't be sent to Alison who would promptly show it to Michael. He would immediately phone the specialist and the fat would be in the fire. No! It must be done by suggestion. Very very carefully done.

Mrs Craig slept soundly and dreamlessly, knowing that it wouldn't be long now before Alison was home once more.

Alison lay in Michael's arms and tried desperately not to think of her mother. Michael had been so wonderful to her; so gentle and patient and adoring. Their love-making had brought her to a new and wonderful world of pleasure she had never believed existed. Now as he slept, his dark curly head against her bare shoulder, his arms even in sleep holding her tightly to him, she loved him so much that to be thinking of anything but him seemed a desecration of their love.

Yet continually her mind turned to her mother. It seemed so wrong to be so deliriously happy while her mother lay, no doubt, awake and utterly miserable, alone. If only she could have been happy in Alison's happiness! If only she could see Michael as Alison saw him. He was so truly wonderful. No girl could ask for a more patient, wonderful and tender lover.

The room was in darkness but the soft moonlight flooding through the window outlined Michael's features, and Alison gazed at him with a heart so full of love that she felt like weeping. She must try not to think of the past, only of their future together; nothing must mar Michael's joy, for he had been so happy and joyful in their wedding night. She wouldn't let him see that her mother lay at the back of her mind, pathetic, needing her and yet having no claim on her now.

Surely it couldn't be long before Mrs Craig gave in. Surely she couldn't refuse to face facts now that Michael and she were really married. When they returned from their honeymoon she would be so glad to see them . . . she *must*. Diane couldn't go on living there indefinitely and Alison couldn't leave her alone in that house. Michael had a furnished flat ready and waiting for them to go back to. It was not very large but he had seen that there was a nice sunny spare room which her mother could have as a bed-sitting-room.

'Later on, we'll get a house and give her a little apartment of her own!' he'd said. 'Then she can have all her own things round her.'

Darling Michael, always so unselfish and considerate of Alison's wishes.

She turned slightly and Michael stirred, opened his eyes and seeing her awake, drew her, with a glad smile, more tightly to him.

'Alison! Darling!'

'I love you so much, Michael!' she whispered.

This time he did not need to be patient for the fierce intensity of her love equalled his own.

Twelve

A t Diane's request Dr McFaddon called in to see Mrs Craig.

'She really doesn't seem a bit well,' Diane said. 'I'm worried about her. Are you absolutely sure there's nothing wrong with her, Doc?'

The old man took off his overcoat and sighed.

'Can't ever be completely sure about anything!' he said. 'But I've never found anything seriously wrong yet. Her heart's as sound as a bell and these aches and pains she has are never in the same place twice. We've had blood tests, of course, and her kidneys and lungs are sound; no cancer or anything like that. In fact, she's a very healthy woman, I'd say.'

'All the same, she seems to have lost a lot of weight. I know she's been worrying dreadfully about Alison. She's got this obsession about Michael and naturally the rift with Alison has made her terribly unhappy. But I did wonder – well, suppose she did have something wrong, something that isn't easy to diagnose. One does hear such awful things about tumours, for instance.'

Dr McFaddon looked at his nurse thoughtfully. She'd proved a very level-headed and sensible nurse and he respected her professional ability. If she really thought something was wrong with the old lady he'd give her another good check-up. But carcinoma – well, there was absolutely no reason to suspect that awful scourge unless she really had lost considerable weight.

It was some months since he'd seen Mrs Craig and now he was deeply shocked at her appearance. Always rather a neat and fastidious woman, she had let her appearance go to pieces. Her face looked old, drawn and grey. She did look as if she'd lost weight, too.

'Well, and how are we today?' he asked cheerfully.

'I'm not at all well, Doctor. I've this awful pain in my stomach. Diane says it's probably only indigestion and I'm not to start getting ideas that there is anything seriously wrong. But every time you pick up a paper, you read these awful cases of people dying, and the doctors don't know until they are dead what was wrong with them.'

Her querulous voice trailed on as he made his examination. She voiced all the doubts Diane had put in her head.

'There's nothing visibly wrong!' Dr McCrail said, much relieved. 'I'll give you a tonic, Mrs Craig. I think it might be a good thing if you could get up and about a bit more, too. Lying in bed isn't good for the system.'

'But I'm not satisfied!' Mrs Craig cried. 'I think I ought to be X-rayed again, Dr McFaddon. Suppose there is something wrong deep inside me. Just because you can't feel anything doesn't prove it isn't there.'

Dr McCrail sighed. Really he wasn't surprised at the request. So many people reading the papers began to get ideas about their various aches and pains and built them up into incurable diseases. It was more surprising that Mrs Craig, a born hypochondriac, hadn't come around to it before.

Still, it might be as well to be on the safe side. One could never be sure with such women whether the pain they complained of was real or imaginary. If it were real *this time*, maybe there could be something there. An X-ray would put her mind at rest.

'Very well!' he said. 'I'll arrange an X-ray for you. But I don't think you have any need to worry, Mrs Craig. Now cheer up. Have you heard from Alison?'

'I have some postcards. She seems to be enjoying herself,' Mrs Craig said. Her voice sounded anything but pleased.

'I think it would be a good idea if you put an end to this nonsense,' Dr McFaddon said sternly. 'Michael Boyce is a very nice young man and an excellent doctor. Alison could

124

have done a great deal worse than marry him, you know.'

Mrs Craig snorted.

'Oh, I know you like him. That's because you're too blind to see what goes on under your very nose!' Mrs Craig said indignantly. She remembered suddenly Diane's enforced promise not to reveal what she knew about Michael. She couldn't do so without revealing the source of her information and then poor dear Diane would lose her job.

'I don't think you ought to cast suspicion on anyone unless you can prove your facts, Mrs Craig!' the old man said sternly. 'Michael is a decent, well-behaved, nice young man. He's been particularly nice about you, and if you'll take my advice you'll accept that room he's offered you and make your peace with them.'

'Never!' Mrs Craig cried. 'I'll never accept that man as Alison's husband. Never!'

Stubborn old woman! Dr McFaddon thought as he left the room and joined Diane downstairs.

'Well?' she asked.

'Can't find anything wrong!' he said, sighing. 'Still, she's determined on an X-ray so I've agreed. Can't do any harm and you can never be sure. Ring the hospital and make an appointment when you get back to surgery, will you, Nurse?'

Diane's eyes filled with satisfaction. She'd done it. Now the first letter could go off to Alison. The sooner the better. And barely before Dr McFaddon had driven away from the house she was up in Mrs Craig's room, dictating a letter.

My dear Alison,

I know that ever since Dr Boyce came to see me that day and determined to take you away from me, you have never believed I was really ill. He made you think I was making it all up when I said I was in pain. So I don't suppose you'll believe me now when I tell you that I've been in quite severe pain for the last few days.

Now, Dr McFaddon has been to see me and it is his view that I ought to have an X-ray. An appointment has been made for me and within a day or two I should know if what I

125

suspect is true. I would have kept this distressing suspicion to myself rather than worry you, but I feel it is my duty to tell you what kind of a man you have chosen to go off with. He was prepared to ignore my symptoms to get you, and this fact alone should show you clearly what sort of a doctor he is.

I will let you know the results of the X-ray and if it is to be the end of my life I would naturally like to see you again before I go. . .

'But I can't send that!' Mrs Craig put down her pen. 'Alison will imagine I've only a few weeks to live.'

'Well, it won't hurt her to worry about you a bit, will it?' Diane said evenly. 'After all, she deserves a little worry after all she has given you.'

'But it seems wrong,' Mrs Craig began, when Diane interrupted firmly.

'You're only saying "if". Now, finish it off, Mrs Craig, in your own words, and I'll post it for you.'

Later, Diane unsealed the envelope and added a short note from herself.

Dear Alison,
I don't think you should worry too much. Dr McFaddon thinks it's wise to be on the safe side but I'm sure there is nothing very seriously wrong and you can rely on me to contact you immediately the results of the X-ray are through. Meanwhile, enjoy your honeymoon, and on no account rush home as there really isn't the slightest proof *of anything in the way of a growth.*
My love to you both,
Diane

Twenty-four hours later Alison opened the letter and read it with mounting horror.

'Michael!'

He came running, hearing the fear in her cry.

White-faced, she handed him the two letters. He frowned

as he read Mrs Craig's, but his face relaxed as he read Diane's note.

'Darling, there isn't the slightest need to worry. Don't you see, this is just another of your mother's wild attempts to drag you back home again.'

Alison's lips tightened.

'I don't see how you can be sure. After all, Dr McFaddon wouldn't have thought an X-ray necessary if there was nothing the matter.'

Michael said patiently:

'It's only a precaution, sweetheart. If she's worrying about herself, this is the best way to put her mind at rest. Diane says quite clearly that there is no "proof" of anything and if there had been the slightest cause for worry, McFaddon would have phoned me. Really, darling, you mustn't let your mother do this to you. You're as white as a ghost!'

'She thinks she has cancer!' Alison cried. 'Suppose it is true, Michael? Suppose we've been wrong all along and she really has been in pain!'

Michael became stern as he heard the hysteria in Alison's voice.

'That's absurd. Neither McFaddon nor I found anything wrong with your mother. This is just another trick to make you go home. You must believe that, Alison.'

'But you can't be sure!' Alison cried. 'If Dr McFaddon were sure, he wouldn't be having her X-rayed.'

'That's just to put her mind at rest!' Michael repeated. 'Now please, darling, *don't* worry! I *know* your mother is all right.'

Alison stared at her husband from eyes grown large with uncertainty.

'How *can* you know, Michael? Very often those things don't show even in an X-ray. I know that's true because I read it somewhere.'

Michael bit his lip.

'All right, so no one can ever be completely sure. There is no absolutely guaranteed proof short of an operation. But we can't all go round thinking we have cancer every time

127

we get a bad pain somewhere, otherwise life would be impossible.'

'So you assume everyone is all right until it is proved they aren't?' Alison questioned quietly.

'If you like to put it that way, yes! If there is any recognizable symptom like a lump or loss of weight, then we check up, then recommend an X-ray or a specialist or, if necessary, an op. But McFaddon would have told me if there had been any symptoms.'

He went to her and tried to take her in his arms, but she moved away deliberately, ignoring the hurt in his eyes.

'Alison, if you don't take my word, then we'll phone McFaddon and you can speak to him.'

Did she doubt him? Alison felt a desperate need for time ... time to think, to sort out the panic and uncertainty into which her mother's letter had thrown her. Could Michael have been wrong all along? He'd never have made a deliberately wrong diagnosis as her mother had suggested, but suppose he had been mistaken?

No, she *must* trust him. What was love if it did not embrace trust? And she needed desperately to believe him. At the same time, she felt she ought to be home, with her mother, help her through this imaginary or real crisis in her life. But to return home would mean to cut short her honeymoon and the days were speeding by so fast. Only this morning, Michael had said:

'When one is as happy as this, time has wings. Only four more days, my darling, and we'll have to go back to reality!'

'Oh, Michael!' She turned and ran into his arms, clinging to him, begging him to try to understand her uncertainty.

He held her fiercely, afraid in some unaccountable fashion that she was slipping away from him.

'I'm *sure* there is nothing to worry about, sweetheart!' he said.

She looked at him helplessly.

'How can you be sure? Even Doc McFaddon isn't sure any more. No one can be sure until after the X-ray.'

Michael frowned. Strictly speaking, she was right. No one

128

could ever be completely certain, and yet Doc had assured him several times there was nothing the matter with the old lady except in her imagination. He, himself, had found nothing wrong. Everything pointed to this being another attempt to bring Alison to heel. Yet while there could be doubt, he was helpless.

'You must do what you think best!' he said quietly, releasing her.

Trust him! cried Alison's heart, but the complete certainty that he was right had left her. If it had not meant disappointing him, hurting him, she would have taken the next train back to Scotland. But how could she? This was her honeymoon...

They had been so close that it wasn't difficult for Michael to divine the thoughts that showed on her face. He turned away, bitterly hurt and miserable.

'We'll go back!' he said briefly.

She ran to him then, flinging her arms round him and crying.

'No, darling, no! We'll wait till we hear the result of the X-ray. I'm not going back.'

He felt a quick rush of joy and he kissed her again and again as if they had only just discovered one another. He felt almost as if he had indeed lost her for a little while and had known how terribly lonely and empty life would be without her.

'I love you too much!' he said at last, letting her go.

They spent the rest of the day as they had planned, visiting Michael's aunt. She was his only relative in England, for his mother and father lived in Kenya. Michael had spent more of his life with his Aunt Elsie than with his own parents, who had wanted a conventional prep and public school English education for him. He had therefore lived with his Aunt Elsie since he was eight years old and had spent only occasional holidays in Kenya with his family.

'You'll love her, Alison!' he had promised his young wife. 'She's been mother and father to me and naturally she's dying to meet you.'

129

Alison had been nervous, for it stood to reason that Aunt Elsie would never think her 'good enough' for Michael.

But within an hour of meeting her, Alison had lost all anxiety. She had never known anyone quite like the elegant, white-haired old lady who lived in a little white doll's house in Hampstead. Years ago, as a young girl, she had lost a leg in a motor accident and now managed to get about fairly well with an artificial leg. She had never married, for the only man she had loved had been killed in the war. Now in her sixties, she lived with her lifelong maid companion, Nellie, and seemed to Alison to be one of the happiest and most complete people she had ever met.

'Of course I'm happy!' Aunt Elsie said as they sat chatting in front of the fire over tea. 'I've been so lucky. Michael has been like my own son and he's always been a great joy to me. You'll understand that, Alison dear! He's a fine person in every way and I'm so very happy to think he's chosen a girl like you for his wife. I was afraid some scheming blonde would get hold of him!'

Alison smiled.

'I'm going to try to be a good doctor's wife. I've no nursing experience, except of course that I've looked after my mother. . .'

Suddenly she found herself telling Aunt Elsie all about her mother. She withheld nothing and the older woman listened patiently. At last she said:

'Of course, I have heard from Michael in his letters about your mother. He wrote very understandingly, Alison, and if I may be frank, I'd like to say that I think he has been very patient. In spite of your mother's antagonism towards him, he is still prepared to offer her a home with you and that isn't what every young husband will do these days, even with a mother-in-law who likes him.'

'I know!' Alison agreed. 'Please don't think I don't appreciate him; I think my mother has behaved very badly indeed, but I'm all she has. I can't walk out on her!'

'My dear, no! I'd never suggest such a thing. I admire you, and so does Michael, for the way you have always

130

cared for your mother. But don't let her separate you two. No one in the world has the right to do that. No one has as great a claim on your time or your love as the man you have married.'

'But if Mother really is ill?' Alison asked. 'What am I to do?'

'Why not wait and see first if there is anything wrong? Naturally, if there were, Michael would be the first person to insist you look after her.'

Her talk with Aunt Elsie did a lot to put Alison's mind at rest. It was clear that here was an intelligent, thoughtful, wordly wise woman who knew Michael through and through. She trusted him completely and Alison's own doubts as to Michael's ability to diagnose her mother's condition seemed disloyal and unworthy by comparison.

She wrote a long, loving letter to her mother. She wrote of the future, saying how eagerly she and Michael were looking forward to moving her into the flat when they returned; how they planned soon to get a house where she could have her own furniture; how much they would need her help. She made no reference to any awful thought that there might be no future, only ending her letter with:

. . .I know the X-ray will be good and that it is a wise thought of Dr McFaddon to have it. Then we will know that it is only a matter of time before you are up and about and quite fit again, Mother. I will phone home tomorrow night to find out if there is any news.

Mrs Craig read the letter and handed it straight to Diane.

'You see, she doesn't care about me any more. He's taken her away completely. She doesn't even care that I might be dying.'

The tears of self-pity flowed easily.

Diane handed back the letter and said:

'Frankly, I'm surprised. I would have thought news such as yours would have brought home any daughter, even if she were on her honeymoon.'

131

Mrs Craig gave Diane an anxious look.

'You don't suppose there really is anything wrong with me? I mean anything serious?'

It was the first time she had really given a thought to this coming X-ray. Quite suddenly, she was terribly afraid. Suppose she really did have some horrible growth? Suppose she really *were* dying?

'I'm frightened!' she cried, clinging to Diane's hand. 'Tell me again what Dr McFaddon said. He doesn't really think there's something wrong? What did he tell you? Maybe he was only trying to make me feel better. Maybe he's known for years and hasn't wanted to tell me.'

Her voice rose hysterically but Diane said nothing to quieten her. Cruelly, she let the hysterical fear mount while her own mind worked furiously as to how she could best turn things to her own way. Frankly, she had hoped Mrs Craig's letter would have brought Alison home. But apparently Michael's influence over her was stronger than she'd imagined. Or maybe they had phoned Dr McFaddon for the facts. She must find out at morning surgery. Meanwhile the X-ray had been fixed for half past two tomorrow.

'Try not to worry!' she said lightly. 'I'll have to go out now. I'll be back in time to get your lunch.'

Mrs Craig burst into tears.

'You mustn't leave me alone, Diane. I can't lie here all morning by myself. I'll go mad thinking about tomorrow. I ought not to be alone.'

'But I have to go to surgery!' Diane said in her cool professional voice.

But Mrs Craig really was hysterical now. Diane hesitated. Maybe she ought not to leave the old girl alone. She might babble anything if one of the neighbours heard her screaming and came in to see what was wrong. She'd better phone Dr McFaddon.

'I'm sorry, Doctor, but she's worked herself into a frenzy and I really think she ought not to be by herself. She's convinced she's dying and I can't reason with her. I'll give her a sedative and come as soon as she's sleeping.'

132

Dr McFaddon sighed and put down the phone. Diane's report on Mrs Craig didn't surprise him. He knew she was quite capable of imagining herself on her death-bed and then really believing it. But Nurse Fellows was sensible and no doubt would cope.

Diane went back to the bedroom.

'Now be quiet and listen, Mrs Craig!' she said sharply. 'I'm going to give you a sleeping-pill. You'll be quite all right in a few minutes and I'll stay with you till then. I really do think Alison ought to have come home. I'm sure she has no idea how upset you are. Perhaps if I phoned her?'

Mrs Craig jumped at the suggestion.

'Yes, yes. Ring her and tell her I need her. She must come back. I want Alison . . . I want Alison . . .'

Diane gave a triumphant little smile. She needed no further excuse to ring Alison. And the telephone number of the hotel was on the notepaper.

She went down and waited impatiently while the trunk call went through.

Alison answered the call in their bedroom. Michael was in the adjoining bathroom shaving and she called:

'It's probably Aunt Elsie!'

But when she heard Diane's voice, her heart jumped in fear.

'I'm terribly sorry to do this on your honeymoon,' Diane was saying. She sounded very close – as clear as if she were in the next room. 'But I don't know what to do about your mother. She's in a terrible state, Alison. I can't seem to give her any reassurance.'

'But what's wrong?' Alison asked, clinging with her free hand to Michael's as he came through to sit on the bed beside her.

'Nothing, really, except that naturally she's very worked up about the X-ray tomorrow. She's so afraid, Alison, and she keeps crying and calling for you. I've given her a sedative but it's really you she wants.'

Alison looked at Michael who quickly took the phone from her.

'Can't you cope, Diane? There's nothing really wrong, is there?'

'I'm doing my best, Michael,' Diane replied. 'But it isn't much good, I'm afraid. She's quite certain in her own mind that there is something to be afraid of and nothing I can say will reassure her.'

'But we'll be back the day after tomorrow,' Michael said. 'Surely she'll be all right until then?' He tried not to see Alison's white, distraught face.

'Yes, of course. But I had to promise I'd ring. She seems to think Alison doesn't care what happens to her and she only promised to quieten down if I rang. The X-ray is tomorrow, incidentally; half past two at the General.'

'Hold on a minute!'

He put his hand over the mouthpiece and turned to his young wife.

'Do you want to speak again, darling? Diane says there's nothing really to worry about. It's just that your mother wanted her to get in touch with you.'

'She needs me!' Alison said. 'Michael, I ought to go to her. I *must* go!'

'I don't think you should!' Michael replied quietly. 'You might only make her more certain there is something to be feared.'

'But she's alone and afraid,' Alison argued. 'I must go, Michael, please!'

Michael did not try to argue with her. Nor would he plead. He handed the phone to Alison and went back to the bathroom.

'Diane, tell Mother I'll come home on the next train. I'll be back in time to take her to hospital myself. Tell her not to worry!'

It was done – the decision was made. Relief flooded through her only to be replaced by misery when she remembered Michael. He'd be so disappointed. Today they had planned to go to Oxford, where he'd taken his degree. He'd been longing to show her round his college.

She ran into the bathroom and, regardless of the cold,

134

stood in her bare feet and flimsy nightie, staring at him.

'Michael, you do understand? I'm so sorry!'

Michael cut himself and swore softly, but he did not turn his head to look at her. He could see her in the glass of the shaving-mirror, but he avoided her eyes. He did not want her to see how hurt and bitterly disappointed he was.

'It's OK!' he said gruffly.

'It isn't! Not if you don't understand!' Alison cried.

'I understand!' Michael replied. He was suddenly too much in love with her to be able to keep his constraint. He turned and faced her, his eyes hard. 'Yes, I understand all right. Your mother didn't succeed in stopping the wedding, but she's succeeded in spoiling our honeymoon. Don't think I didn't know you lay awake half of last night worrying about her. She's been like a ghost between us ever since you got that damned letter.'

His violence frightened and appalled her.

'Michael, that isn't true! And I couldn't help worrying. So would you if it had been your Aunt Elsie.'

'On the contrary. If I knew she was faking I'm damned if I'd let Aunt Elsie spoil my honeymoon.'

Alison was now angry. Two bright pink spots stained her cheeks. She looked lovely and completely desirable but he wouldn't touch her. If he had been able to do so they might not have quarrelled so bitterly.

'Faking? That's what you've said all along. But you might be wrong. I don't say you are, but you *might*!' she flung at him. 'Even you yourself admitted no one could be sure. Well, until I'm sure, I can't stay here enjoying life as if nothing at all were the matter. I thought you understood. I thought you loved me enough to understand.'

'I love you enough to mind that you care a damn sight more for your mother's feelings than you do for me!' Michael flung back. He regretted the words but his pride would not let him take them back. They were true, anyway.

'You're just jealous! Childishly jealous!' Alison flared at him, desperately near to tears.

'Very well, I am! So go back to Mother. Go back and find

135

out for yourself how genuine she is this time. But don't expect me to come with you.'

Until that moment he'd been perfectly willing to go with her. He wouldn't have dreamt of letting her make the long journey alone, of being parted from her.

'I don't *want* you with me!' Alison cried, and rushed out of the room, banging the door behind her.

Michael put down the razor he still held in a shaking hand and stared at the closed door white-faced and frightened. They were quarrelling – and over that mother of hers. It was mad, crazy, when for months he had forced himself to be tactful, understanding. But this time she had tried him too far, ruining the last days of his honeymoon.

'Damn, hell and blast!' he swore softly. He knew he couldn't leave it like this. His anger was subsiding but he felt so wretchedly miserable that he was afraid of what he might do. It would be so easy to take her in his arms and plead with her to stay. Yet, even if she agreed, what pleasure would they find in each other for the last forty-eight hours, each knowing Alison wished to be somewhere else. No, he wouldn't plead.

Dressing hurriedly and without care, Alison's anger also subsided. She, too, was desperately unhappy. To be quarrelling with Michael, whom she loved so truly and so deeply! She no longer wanted to go. She couldn't bear to go without him. Nothing else mattered as much as he did and, poor darling, he had every right to be hurt and disappointed.

If he asks me to stay, I will, she thought. Let him ask me. Please let him ask me.

But he didn't. He came in quietly and put his arms round her. She clung to him, tears pouring down her cheeks.

'I'm sorry, darling!' he said. 'I oughtn't to have spoken to you like that.'

'If you want me to, I'll stay!' Alison choked.

'No!' His voice was sharp, resisting the temptation to give way, to plead, to keep her. 'No, you go. I'll spend a couple of days with Aunt Elsie. She'll be pleased to see me. I might drive her to Oxford. She used to enjoy visiting me there.'

136

Alison stiffened. In her turn, she was now jealous and hurt. So Michael didn't really mind the separation so much. He was prepared for her to go without a fight. Maybe it was better this way. Her mother needed her far more than Michael did!

'I'll ring you from home tomorrow evening,' she said. 'When will you be back?'

'As planned, on Friday,' Michael said, forcing a lightness to his tone of voice. 'I'll go straight to the flat.'

'I'll be there to meet you,' Alison promised. It was a promise she was destined not to keep.

Thirteen

'Didn't I tell you she'd come back?' Diane said with barely concealed triumph as she tucked Mrs Craig into her freshly made bed and plumped up the pillows. 'Now it's up to you to keep her with you.'

'But how?' Mrs Craig asked, alternating between satisfaction and fear. After all, Alison might be furiously angry with her if the X-ray proved there was nothing wrong. But she was ill. . .she *was*. Only not too ill! she reminded herself. She didn't want an incurable disease.

Diane had it all worked out.

'You must just refuse to go for the X-ray. Keep Alison here as long as you can. If you can keep her away from her husband for a few weeks, his influence over her will weaken and you can make her see what kind of man he really is.'

'But I must have my X-ray!' Mrs Craig said, completely confused now. 'It's all been arranged. Besides, suppose there is something wrong—'

'Dr McFaddon only fixed it up for you because *you* were worried. Besides, a really good doctor ought to be able to diagnose your trouble without an X-ray. I should think the sensible thing for you to do is to leave McFaddon and register with another doctor, one you really feel you can trust. If the new one thinks an X-ray is necessary, well, you can always have it. But that need not be for a week or two.'

'But you agreed with me that I really was ill,' the old woman faltered. 'Now you say you think I'm all right.'

Diane concealed her irritation with an effort. She'd had to change her attitude to suit the prevailing circumstances and obviously since the X-ray would show the old lady as fighting fit, Alison wouldn't stay home long after the result was out! No, this way was far better. Keep Alison in doubt, keep her worried, keep her away from Michael so that he got fed up with it; lonely, embittered. Then her own chance would come.

'No, of course I don't think you're perfectly well. I've said all along I thought your attacks were quite genuine. But I'm sure – all the more sure having nursed you for the last few days – that it's probably some bug you've picked up which flares up from time to time whenever your resistance is low. That could account for the pains in your leg and back and for your headaches and depression, too. A more modern and up-to-date doctor than McFaddon might find it out.'

Mrs Craig gave a sigh of relief. The thought of being at death's door had frightened her. Even at the cost of having Alison back, she didn't want to be dying! This was a far better 'illness' to be suffering from and Diane was probably quite right. McFaddon was old and out of date. Diane had been in a big London hospital and would see this. She ought to have got rid of him years ago.

'Yes, yes, you're right, Diane!' she said with mounting satisfaction. 'I'm sure you're right.'

'Of course, it wouldn't be wise to let Alison know it isn't quite so serious after all. We must go on letting her believe it is a matter of life and death. Otherwise she'll just run off and leave you for good.'

'It's terrible the way that man has changed her,' Mrs Craig said fiercely. 'At one time, she was gentle and sweet and loving. Now she's hard and all her love for me has gone.'

'But it will return!' Diane said soothingly. 'I'm sure she's a good girl and a dutiful daughter at heart. If only we can succeed in keeping her away from the bad influence, she'll be herself again.'

It was quite late before Alison found herself in a taxi travelling from the station to her home. It had been a long, tedious and miserable journey for her. Each mile which passed, separating her still further from Michael, made her the more wretched and uncertain. She ought to have stayed with him. It was only two days, and what purpose was served in coming home before the X-ray was done? Only as a comfort to her mother and for this she was making Michael unhappy and losing two precious days of their honeymoon which could never be recaptured.

Her mood changed and once again she felt at war with her husband. He ought to have understood that she *had* to go. Her mother might be dying. It was a terrible and ghastly possibility and surely, if he loved her, Michael could not want to be selfish on such a terrible occasion.

But she knew in her heart it was not selfishness. Had Michael really believed her mother to be ill he'd have been the first to rush her home. No, it was this conviction of his that she wasn't ill at all. Faking! That's the word he had used. As if anyone would pretend over such a momentous thing as their own life! And the X-ray. Surely Dr McFaddon wouldn't have agreed to it unless he really believed it necessary. Nor would Diane, a trained nurse, have asked her to go back unless she felt her mother really needed her.

I had to come, she told herself, mile after mile. But she did not entirely convince herself and the knowledge that tonight, four hundred miles would separate her from Michael was so distressing that only by a great effort did she restrain her tears.

Their parting at the railway station had been silent and painful. Both had tried to make casual conversation. Both had been wretched at the thought of parting. Both wished desperately to relent – Alison to stay with him, Michael to go with her. But with each, pride took first place. When the whistle finally blew, they clung together in a swift, desperate kiss and the next moment the train was moving away and Michael's figure receding.

Now, in the taxi, she tried in vain to comfort herself. The day after tomorrow they would be together again. She would go to the new flat in the afternoon, light the fire, cook her first meal for him. Everything would be done to make it a wonderful homecoming, a wonderful welcome. . .

Her thoughts turned once more to her mother and she

prayed silently and devoutly that there was nothing seriously wrong.

Diane opened the front door. For a moment, her bright expression of welcome faded.

'Michael not with you?' she asked involuntarily.

Alison walked through into the hall.

'No! He is staying the last two days with his aunt. It seemed pointless him coming back to an empty flat. Diane, how is Mother?'

Diane's face took on a look of grave concern.

'She's not too good, I'm afraid, Alison. I think it's so terrible that you should have had to cut short your honeymoon like this. And there's always the chance there is nothing wrong with her at all.'

Alison felt irritated suddenly by Diane's concern for her happiness. At the same time, she was afraid again.

'Then you really believe she is ill?'

'Oh, I didn't say that!' Diane replied swiftly. 'But *she* thinks so, Alison. You know what she thinks is the matter with her – and nowadays, one hates to accuse people of lying about such things because one can never be sure. But the fact is, she believes it and now something worse has happened. She's refusing to have an X-ray.'

Alison looked at Diane in surprise.

'Refusing? But that's mad! The only way to put her mind at rest and for all of us to be sure is to be X-rayed. She must go!'

'Well, she won't!' Diane replied. 'Obviously she is afraid to know the worst. She would rather not know. Of course, I've argued with her until I'm blue in the face but it hasn't done any good.'

Alison felt a swift rush of concern for Diane. She must have had a terrible week and she, Alison, owed her a lot for being here at all. Later, she must find some way to repay Diane for those precious days with Michael. But for her, they might have had no honeymoon at all!

'I'll talk to Mother,' she said. 'Hasn't Doc McFaddon tried?'

'She won't see him!'

'Won't *see* him? But why?'

'She says she's lost faith in him; that he's too old and doesn't understand her case.'

'But she adores him!' Alison cried, too surprised to think coherently. 'Why, he brought me into the world, he was Father's doctor, too. Mother would never have anyone else.'

'Well, you talk to her, Alison. Try to make her see reason. Try to convince her she isn't really seriously ill at all. Maybe she'll believe you.'

Alison took off her coat and, tired though she was, she went straight upstairs to Mrs Craig's room.

At the sight of her daughter, Mrs Craig burst into tears. She was genuinely so happy to see Alison back. It had seemed more like ten weeks than ten days since she had been in the room beside her.

Alison felt tears in her own eyes. Impulsively she ran forward and clasped her mother in her arms.

'Don't go away again. Don't leave me!' Mrs Craig cried. 'I've needed you so terribly, Alison!'

'There, Mother, I'm back now!' Alison said to comfort her. 'Look, borrow my handkerchief. What a couple of old sillies we are to be crying. We ought to be laughing to see each other again.'

Mrs Craig sniffed.

'I've nothing to laugh about, Alison. You wouldn't feel like laughing with a possible death sentence hanging over your head.'

'That's nonsense, Mother!' Alison replied, concealing her own fear and remembering Diane's caution to be firm. 'I'm quite sure there's nothing wrong. Doc McFaddon would have sent for me if he'd had the slightest fear that—'

'That man!' Mrs Craig broke in vehemently. 'I don't trust him an inch any more, Alison. He's too old now to be a good doctor. I'm going to get a new man.'

'Mother, that's just silly!' Alison argued impatiently. 'Doc McFaddon has dealt with your case for years. Now he wants this X-ray to put all our minds at rest and you turn against him and call him old-fashioned.'

142

'I'm not having the X-ray!' Mrs Craig said stubbornly.

'But you *must*!' Alison said. 'That's why I've come back now, Mother, so I could go with you to the hospital tomorrow.'

'Well, I'm not going, Alison, so you might as well save your breath. I told Dr McFaddon so on the telephone and he said he'd have Diane cancel the appointment. You can't make me go and I won't!'

Alison sat down abruptly on the chair by the bed. Her legs felt weak and she was suddenly deathly tired and unequal to this battle. But she must try.

'Look, Mother, you must be sensible about this. We can't all go on worrying for ever that there is something really seriously wrong. You owe it to yourself and to me to find out. I know it's a bit frightening, but I'm quite quite sure that there isn't anything to be frightened about. Why, if Dr McFaddon really thought you had some. . .some awful thing, he'd have *insisted* on the X-ray, wouldn't he?'

Mrs Craig saw the sense in this and it further lightened her heart. Of course she needn't fear she was dying. Diane was perfectly right.

'Then there's no need for an X-ray,' she said.

'But, Mother, it's necessary to reassure yourself. You can't live happily with that kind of fear at the back of your mind.'

'I'd much rather *not* know,' Mrs Craig retorted. 'And I'm surprised that *you* should be so eager to hear bad news about me, Alison. I suppose that's all I can expect now you and that man—'

'Mother!' Alison's voice broke in sharply. 'I am Michael's wife and I won't listen to you speaking against him, do you understand?'

'Very well, I won't! But it's clear you don't really love me any more. Maybe you'll be sorry when I'm dead that you treated me so unkindly at the end.'

'Mother!'

Alison jumped up and walked up and down the room. It was horrible to hear her mother talk like this. And it was so unfair. It was love for her mother which had torn her away from Michael's side, on their honeymoon.

'Doesn't it mean anything that I've left him to come here tonight?' she asked, bitterly hurt.

'Left him?' Mrs Craig's hopes were raised. 'You've left him? Oh, Alison, I knew you'd come to your senses in the end. I knew you'd find him out.'

Alison stared at her mother white-faced.

'Mother, I meant only that I'd left Michael alone in London, to come here to be with you for a few days. Of course I haven't left him for good. I'm his wife. And I love him with my whole heart.'

The corners of Mrs Craig's mouth turned down.

'So you don't care. I might as well be dead. I've no one in the world but you and I mean nothing to you any more. I don't know why you did come home at all.'

'To be with you tomorrow!' Alison said desperately. 'You must go, Mother. Even if you don't want to know the truth, *I* do. I love you enough to want to be sure that you are all right!'

'You've never believed I was ill – not since that man came into my house and turned you against me. You don't believe I'm ill now. Well, go back to him. I'd rather die alone than have you here checking up on me as a *duty!*'

Alison was nearly crying with exasperation.

'It's because I love you so much that I am so worried about you!' she cried. 'You must believe that, Mother.'

'Well, we'll see what the new doctor has to say. If he really thinks it necessary then maybe I will be X-rayed.'

'But what new doctor? When is he coming?' Alison asked anxiously.

'I haven't decided on one yet!' Mrs Craig said, enjoying Alison's concern. 'Diane has promised to bring me a list of all the ones round about. Then I'll choose one and maybe he'll be able to discover what is the matter with me.'

'But, Mother . . .' She broke off, suddenly realizing the futility of arguing. No doubt Diane had already said everything there was to say about the inadvisability of changing

144

doctors; about the dangers of delaying an X-ray if there really was anything seriously wrong. How could she possibly make her mother see this without frightening her? If only she had liked and accepted Michael, what better person to try to convince her. But obviously, despite the fact that he was now her son-in-law, she felt as antagonistic about him as before.

'Mother, I do want to talk to you about something else. The future, our future. When I left to be married, you were so upset you refused to answer me when I asked you which day you would like to move into the flat.'

Mrs Craig pursed her lips.

'It's no good pretending, Alison. I told you then and I still mean it, I won't live in the same house as that man.'

'Mother, please!' Alison begged. 'It's my home. You know I can't be happy unless you come, too.'

'You should have thought of that before you married him!' Mrs Craig quoted Diane who had used the same words two nights earlier when they discussed the question.

'But you can't live here by yourself!'

'I must!' Mrs Craig said in a martyred tone. 'I'll just have to pull myself round the house. I don't pretend I'm looking forward to it, ill as I feel, but I'd rather do that than live under the same roof with that man.'

Alison gripped her hands together, trying to keep calm. She felt that if her mother called Michael 'that man' again, she would scream.

'That's quite ridiculous. Even if you won't talk to him, at least I would be there to look after you. You can stay in your own room and I'll bring up your meals. I'm ordering the removal van to come at the weekend. Michael said he would help me pack everything up. What you don't need can go into storage.'

'I won't go and you can't make me!' cried Mrs Craig.

'You can't stay here alone. It's not as if you were well!' Alison tried to be patient. 'And you know I can't stay with you, Mother. It's no good hoping I will because I can't. You are free to come to me and I don't think it fair that you should try to make things harder for me.'

145

'You've made your choice, Alison!' Mrs Craig said. 'I told you that on your wedding day. I knew I'd lost you then. No girl who really loved her mother would ever have been married without her there. Not that I called what you had a wedding service.'

The fact that she privately agreed only made Alison argue more fiercely that it was not so. Finally she burst into tears and for the first time Mrs Craig weakened.

'Don't upset yourself,' she said in a more kindly voice. 'Don't you see, dear, that even if you have made a terrible mistake, it can always be put right. You don't have to go on living with him.'

Alison stood up, tears still running down her cheeks.

'Don't you understand yet, Mother, that I don't want to leave him? I love him. He's my husband. I'm crying because I wish so much he was here.'

She turned and ran out of the room. Downstairs, Diane sat in the kitchen. She looked at Alison with every appearance of concern.

'Bad as all that?' she asked, patting Alison's shoulder and handing her a cup of tea.

'It's hopeless!' Alison cried despairingly. 'It isn't just the X-ray business, it's the whole question of the future. Mother absolutely refuses to come to the flat. What am I going to do, Diane? I can't forcibly drag her there, can I? And I know Michael is going to hate all this fuss. Yet I can't leave her alone.'

'I wish I could help you out by staying with her,' Diane said sweetly. 'But honestly, I just can't, Alison. I'm very fond of your mother, but the business of coping with her as well as having my work to do is too much.'

'I don't expect it of you, Diane. Why should you? She isn't your mother.'

'That's half the trouble. She doesn't really want *me* here. It is you she wants. It's pathetic how much she loves you and depends on you.'

Alison drank a little of the hot tea and felt calmer.

'It's my own fault. Michael was right. For years I have

let her depend on me for everything. Now she has no one else.'

'I don't think Michael should criticize all you have done for Mrs Craig. After all, when your father died, it was your duty to care for her. I think you are to be praised, Alison, not blamed. Naturally Michael is jealous of the time you give your mother. Like any man, he wants you all to himself. I'm afraid it isn't going to be easy, my dear. You're bound to hurt one or the other.'

'Perhaps I ought not to have married him,' Alison cried with a new feeling of apprehension and misery. 'I've hurt him already and I know he doesn't understand my rushing back like this.'

'He is a doctor!' Diane argued. 'He ought to understand, Alison. After all, he professes to be a psychiatrist. I think he was wrong to rush you into this wedding before your mother had agreed. It makes everything so much more complicated for you now. How *can* you leave her alone?'

'I don't know!' Alison sighed deeply. 'But I wanted to be married as much as Michael. I was so sure Mother would give way in the end.'

'Perhaps Michael would agree to come and live here. After all, a furnished flat like yours can always be rc-let. Michael could move in here.'

Alison was silent. She could foresee the scene her mother would make: 'That man under my roof? Never!' and she could also foresee what Michael would feel. Naturally he wanted his own home, a place where he was head of the house. He wouldn't want to come here as an unwelcome guest. She said as much to Diane.

'Well, I would have thought it the only solution,' Diane said in her friendly, sympathetic voice. 'Surely he can't expect you just to walk out on your own mother?'

'I feel as if I'm being torn in two!' Alison said despairingly. 'I'm so worried about her, Diane. Do *you* think it is serious? How can one know? If I thought there were really nothing at all wrong, I'd never have left Michael. I'd just give Mother no alternative but to come with us.'

147

Diane was silent, her mind working furiously. A good thing Alison was so credulous. Anyone could see the old lady was putting it on. No wonder Michael was fed up! But she must foster this belief of Alison's that there could be something seriously wrong. Otherwise she might walk out and leave her mother and then there would be no hope for her, Diane. As it was the chances were none too good. She'd hoped that by now Alison and Michael would have quarrelled much more lastingly. The wedding, for instance. Diane had never believed Alison would go through with it without Mrs Craig's approval, or at least consent. The girl had shown more gumption than she'd given her credit for. Then there was the question of the furnished flat they had rented. The cards had been stacked against Diane, for who would have thought that a charming, self-contained, reasonably priced apartment would have fallen vacant a week before the wedding! With the existing housing shortage, too.

Diane sighed, an exasperated and irritated sigh. It was proving a harder job than she had supposed, but her determination to win the game somehow had never slackened. Rather it had increased with every fresh obstacle. Another woman might have given in the day Alison and Michael were married. But she was completely unscrupulous, without regard to moral issues when they conflicted with her own desires. And she wanted Michael at all costs, at any price, no matter who suffered in the process.

'I must go and pack!' she said, leaving Alison's last question unanswered. 'Ring me if there is anything I can do. I wish I could be more hopeful!'

An hour later Diane had gone, taking with her a very beautiful make-up set Alison had chosen with care in London as a thank-you present for caring for her mother.

'I can never repay you, Diane. You don't know how wonderful those ten days were.'

Jealousy twisted Diane's mouth into a thin, bitter line. Even Alison noticed and thought: I ought not to have mentioned my own happiness. She is miserable and unhappy

148

and maybe she is remembering her own honeymoon! Poor Diane!

Poor Diane thought only: And if I have my way, those will be the only ten days you'll have!

Fourteen

Michael collected the suitcases from the back of the car and felt in his pocket for his latchkey. His face was glowing from the cold and an inner excitement. He could see the lights shining from the sitting-room window and the thought that in a few seconds he would hold Alison in his arms again was making his heart beat furiously.

He'd been utterly miserable without her and although Aunt Elsie had done her best to keep him entertained, both had known that his heart had gone back to Scotland with Alison, and but for his stupid pride he would have followed her there the day after she had gone.

Crazy! Michael told himself for the hundredth time. As if pride matters when love is at stake!

He fitted his key in the lock and pushed the door open with his foot.

'Darling!' he shouted, uncaring of who else in the adjoining flats might hear. 'I'm home!'

There was a tantalizing smell of cooking as he opened his front door. He smiled, realizing that this was the first meal he would have in his own home, cooked by his new young wife.

The kitchen door opened and Michael's smile changed to a look of annoyance. What was Diane doing here? Surely she must realize that this homecoming was one when two and not three were required. He noticed the apron and looked at her with surprise.

'Welcome home, Michael!'

'Where's Alison?'

Diane tried not to show her annoyance. 'I'm frightfully sorry, Michael, but she isn't here.'

Michael frowned. 'Isn't here!' he repeated. 'But why? When is she coming? Where is she?'

'She'll be along later!' Diane said. 'Now take your coat off and sit down by the fire and get warm. I'll bring you a drink and tell you all about it.'

Too disappointed to argue, Michael took off his coat and walked over to the fire. Disappointment was so acute that he felt a hard lump in his throat which forbade speech.

Diane came back into the room with a large whisky and soda. Michael took it and drank it quickly.

'Now, let's have it!' he said sharply.

Diane smoothed her tight jersey tunic dress and sat on the arm of the chair, her long legs crossed, and toyed with her own glass.

'I really am sorry, Michael,' she said slowly. 'I knew you'd be upset and I told Alison she really *ought* to be here to meet you. After all, *you* should come first, but I suppose you can't talk other people round to your way of thinking. Alison seems to feel she must be with her mother and she's counting on your understanding.'

Michael bit his lip. 'This is going to take quite a bit of understanding!' he said sharply. 'She told me last night on the phone that the X-ray is off. What has happened today to make it imperative for her to be with her mother? She's been with her all day!'

Anger was now replacing disappointment and was uppermost.

'I know! I told her you'd feel this way. Any man would. In my view you've been too easy-going about your mother-in-law! Frankly, I think it's high time someone had the courage to tell her where to get off. It's this new doctor Mrs Craig is seeing. Apparently she telephoned him herself and he agreed to call at six this evening. Of course, she's insisting Alison should be there when he comes and Alison, of course, gave way. I offered to be there, but Alison wouldn't hear of it.'

She omitted to tell Michael that Alison had considered it her duty to stay herself so she could establish once and for all what was wrong with her mother.

151

'I've got to know, Diane, for Michael's sake as much as mine. Once I have his word nothing is wrong, then I can be firm with Mother and nothing, *nothing* she can say or do will make me leave Michael again.'

'But why now? Good God, it's six o'clock!' Michael cried in exasperation. 'Alison knew I'd be home by six. I told her last night. Surely this doctor could have come earlier.'

'No doubt,' Diane agreed smoothly. 'But your fond mother-in-law presumably wished to keep you and Alison apart and managed to make the appointment for this time. She's no fool, Michael. Unfortunately, Alison believed her when she said it was the only time this man could come.'

'Who is he? What does McFaddon say about it?' Michael questioned.

Diane filled Michael's glass and her own and sat down again. 'Dr McFaddon can't do anything about it. Mrs Craig is perfectly entitled to change her doctor if she wishes. I gather he was up yesterday to see her and there was a bit of a row. Naturally, he isn't taking it too well. He's been the family doctor for years now. But Mrs Craig was adamant and there's nothing he can do.'

'Who is the new man?' Michael asked.

'A young man called Snipe. He lives over on the new estate, I gather. Dr McFaddon said he was only just out of medical school and not at all the right type to deal with a hypochondriac like Mrs Craig. He warned her, but all she said was that the new doctor might have some new ideas. Certainly he, Dr McFaddon, never found out what was wrong.'

'Damn it, there isn't anything wrong!' Michael stood up and charged round the room in exasperation. 'Why can't Alison see that?'

'Perhaps she doesn't want to see it,' Diane said smoothly. 'Perhaps she would rather not face the truth! It would force her into a choice between you and her mother and, in my view, Alison has never been willing to make that choice.'

Michael looked at Diane and his anxiety showed plainly in the lines of his face.

'You honestly think that if I forced her to choose between us she wouldn't come to me?'

Diane looked away from the direct question in Michael's eyes. Privately, she was sure that if put to the choice, Alison would go to Michael. She was in love, and what woman would give up the man she loved, her own husband, for an ailing mother who might not be ailing at all? But she wasn't going to say this.

'I think you should be careful, Michael. Alison is very young, immature in a way. I don't think she probably feels things as deeply as, say, you or I do. You rather swept her off her feet, you know.'

Michael took a deep breath, suddenly desperately afraid. In a nice way, Diane was saying that Alison's love for him was not as deep or strong or lasting as his for her. It was true, too, that he'd swept her off her feet. He'd had to, to wake her up to the fact that she was wasting her life. But maybe she was already regretting it. Maybe she enjoyed her life of martyrdom to that mother of hers. Maybe she got some kind of satisfaction from her mother's dependence.

'I'll never give her up!' He spoke his thoughts aloud. 'I'm not going to let her throw her life away. I love her, Diane. And I *know* she loves me.'

'No doubt she does, Michael, in her own way. It just doesn't happen to be your way – or mine, come to that. Of course, she wanted to be here tonight. But she didn't want it enough. When I offered to drop in and cook a meal for you and explain, she jumped at it. And what happens later, Michael? Is all your married life going to be like this? She can't live in two homes very well, can she?'

'But that's absurd,' Michael argued. 'When her mother moves in here she can look after us both.'

'But Mrs Craig *won't* move in here,' Diane said quietly, pointedly. 'And you can't make her, Michael. So what happens now? Where will Alison make her home?'

Michael looked at his companion white-faced.

'With me, of course!'

'Yes, that's what she *should* do. But *will* she? This evening

153

seems to me to point to the future. You'll have to be firm or else the rest of your life will be like this, until the old girl dies, anyway.'

She's right, Michael thought. I've been too weak. I must put my foot down once and for all. Alison has got to choose. I'm not sharing my wife with anyone!

'When will she be here?' he asked Diane.

'No doubt when her mother doesn't need her any more,' Diane said hurtfully. 'Cheer up, Michael. I've got a good dinner for you. Have another drink first. There is time!'

Michael knew he ought not to have any more whisky until he'd eaten something. He'd left London at six after a very scanty breakfast and had been driving for twelve hours, stopping only once for some sandwiches and a cup of coffee. Now the two strong whiskies Diane had given him had begun to make him feel light-headed.

But before he could refuse Diane had handed him a glass and, too tired suddenly to argue, he drank it slowly, the warmth returning and with it a slow deep anger with Alison for hurting him. He'd been so desperate to see her he hadn't even stopped for a meal! And having driven across the country like some mad thing, she couldn't even be bothered to come here to meet him. Well, it wasn't good enough. Diane thought so, too. She was a good sort, Diane. But for her he'd have come home to a cold flat and no food. And a fat lot Alison, his wife, cared. All she cared about was her mother. . .

None too sure of what he was doing, Michael ate his meal. His head was beginning to clear when he had finished, but a large brandy Diane insisted he needed to warm him up and finish off the meal made him sleepy and hazy again. He'd meant to telephone Alison to say he'd arrived, but somehow he wasn't sure he could walk a straight line to the phone. Mustn't let Nurse Fellows see he was tight. Never do!

'Michael!'

He frowned and tried to concentrate his gaze on Diane's face, but it swam before him.

'Michael, listen! There might be a way to make Alison see sense.'

154

'Make her?' Michael repeated. 'But how?'

Diane sat on the arm of his chair and risked touching his dark curly hair with a long white finger. He didn't appear to notice.

'Well, you could make her jealous. I think that might do the trick. After all, it's one thing to string you along when she knows for sure you're waiting to pick up the left-overs. It's another to be unsure whether you love her or not.'

'Got a point there!' Michael said thickly. 'But how? Never looked at another woman seriously since I met Alison. 'Sides, she's not the jealous type!'

Diane laughed. 'Nonsense! Every woman is jealous. Besides, remember the time her mother told all those lies about us, you and me, Michael? Alison came rushing round to find out what was up. Maybe if she found us here together – well, a bit closer together – she might begin to wonder again. I'm dead sure she wouldn't go home again. She'd stay here with you the night.'

He didn't want to be left alone. He wanted Alison here, with him. She was his wife and she ought to be here. Diane said so, and she knew. A woman of experience. Probably understood her own sex better than he did.

He grinned. 'S'OK by me, if you think it will work.'

'I'm sure it will!' Diane said. 'She'll be here soon, I expect. Put your arms round me, Michael. I could sit on your knee, couldn't I?'

Michael blinked two or three times, trying to sober himself up. He couldn't think very clearly at all. Was it one or two brandies he'd had? Better not have any more.

He felt Diane's weight on his lap and a moment later her soft bare white arms were round his neck. They felt nice, cool yet warm and loving. He could smell her perfume and it seemed familiar. Not Alison's, yet he was doing this for Alison. Somehow or other, he'd got to do this for Alison.

'Now kiss me!' Diane said. 'We must make it realistic, Michael.'

A moment later, her mouth was against his own and he was kissing her. She was exciting, soft and warm and responsive, like Alison who should have been here in her place. His mind felt hopelessly confused and he knew he ought to drink some black coffee and sober up. That last brandy had been one too many! This wasn't Alison – it was Diane! He ought not to be kissing her, yet it was she who was kissing him . . .

'Diane!' he protested, but she seemed not to hear him. The next moment he heard the door open and Diane sprang up.

'Alison, it's you!' As though Alison were the last person in the world she expected to see.

Alison stood in the doorway, rooted to the floor. Her face was chalk-white and all the tension, tiredness and excitement of the day mounted to her head so that she felt faint and swayed on her feet. She blinked hard, trying to rid herself of the horrible picture of Diane in Michael's arms. Her eyes went from Diane's flushed, sparkling, cruel face to Michael's. He was still in the armchair, staring at her with a puzzled frown as if he, too, had not expected to see her.

For a moment, no one spoke. They were like statues in a child's game of tableaux.

Then Diane said: 'I'm sorry, Alison. We had no idea you would be here so soon.'

'Didn't think you were ever coming!' Michael mumbled with remembered jealousy and disappointment. 'Should have been here to meet me. Not fair!'

Alison's voice was icy. 'Not fair! Yet you seem to have found a perfectly good substitute for me. I've been pretty silly, haven't I? My mother was right after all. You are a cheat, Michael, and no good. And you could do this, *this*, when we've only been married two weeks!'

Tears threatened, bringing a hard lump to her throat. She was so shocked and horrified that even now this seemed more like a nightmare than reality. But Diane's next words only confirmed her fears.

'Don't blame Michael too much, Alison. After all, if you'd been here, it might never have happened. We never meant it to happen.'

156

Alison swung on her, white with anger. 'You, Diane! You professed to be my friend. I trusted you and believed in you. I might have known. You're no better than Michael. I hate you – I hate both of you. I never want to see either of you again.'

She turned and slammed the door hard behind her. Michael, momentarily sobered, jumped to his feet and hurried towards the door, but Diane laid a restraining hand on his arm.

'Don't be a fool, Michael! Don't you see our plan has worked? Alison is jealous now; it's just what you wanted, remember? Let her go back to her mother. Let her think she has lost you. In a day or two you can explain and she'll come running back to you.'

Michael hesitated. 'But suppose she doesn't? Poor darling, she looked so hurt, so appalled. It isn't fair. I don't like it, Diane.'

'Now don't be a fool, Michael,' Diane repeated. 'So far you've made a mess of everything. Leave it to me this time. I know women, and Alison in particular. Let me handle this.'

Michael bit his lip, uncertain and wretchedly unhappy. It was true he'd made a mess of everything up to now. Maybe Diane did know best. Certainly *he* wasn't sure of the best way to bring Alison to her senses. But this. . .well, it seemed so cruel, and so final. How could they explain when the time came? And suppose Alison refused to believe them! He might lose her altogether, before their marriage had really begun.

'I must go to her!' he told Diane.

'You'll regret it!' Diane shot back at him. 'If you are weak now, she will always have you just where she wants you, tied to Mrs Craig's apron-strings the way she is. Is that what you want? A life spent under your mother-in-law's domination? It won't be easy, Michael. You'll have to live in her house, do as she says, take your holidays when she wants. Alison won't really be your wife at all.'

Michael heard and paused. He was now so deathly tired that he couldn't reason with any clarity. Alison's stricken, shocked face was haunting him, and yet Diane's words, sharp, clear and to the point, held him back.

'Poor sweet, you look worn out!' He heard Diane's voice, soft now and solicitous. 'Why not pop off to bed and when you wake up, you'll be able to think more clearly. It's always a mistake to rush into action before you've thought out what is best to do. In the morning it will all seem clear.'

Would it? Michael wondered, as, obediently, he allowed Diane to lead him towards the bedroom door. If only he weren't so tired, so confused. He couldn't argue any more. He just wanted to sleep.

'You going home now?' he asked Diane.

Diane made a noncommittal noise which sounded like a 'yes'.

'Goodnight then. Sorry about all this. Don't see why you should have to get involved. Damn shame!' Michael murmured, and disappeared into the bedroom, closing the door behind him. When Diane looked in five minutes later he was lying on the bed, fully dressed and sound asleep.

She smiled, a slow feline smile of satisfaction.

At last, at last! she thought triumphantly. Alison wasn't going to forgive this evening in a hurry. The greater the love for Michael, the greater the disillusionment and hurt. Tomorrow, no doubt, Michael would be all for rushing round to explain. But before that happened, she must give her explanation. And after that, Alison wouldn't listen to Michael.

She found her coat and, slinging it over her shoulders, hurried out into the night. It had been raining and the pavements were shining and the air wet. Diane neither noticed nor cared. She walked hurriedly, smoothly, like a jungle cat, looking neither right nor left. Within ten minutes, she was ringing the bell at Alison's door.

Alison, lying on her bed, sobbing with the deep gasping sobs that seemed to well up from her very heart, heard the ring and sprang off the bed. Michael! He had come to say he was sorry, to apologize, to explain. If only he could convince her that it had meant nothing, that he and Diane . . .But what could explain their being in one another's arms? Did she want to forgive him? Not to do so meant to face a life without him for always.

The bell rang again, insistently, and because she wanted more than anything in the world to be reconciled with her husband she went downstairs to open the door.

She gave a little shiver of disappointment and distaste when she saw the older girl standing there.

'Please, Alison. Let me come in and explain.'

'I've no wish to hear anything at all from you!' Alison said scathingly.

'I know, I do understand how you feel. But I owe it to Michael. You must listen to me, Alison. Please let me come in.'

With some strange detached part of her mind, Alison noted how attractive Diane looked. There was a smooth sophistication about her even with her hair wet with rain and that coat slung around her shoulders. The look came from within, a kind of glow. Was this what Michael found so irresistible?

She stepped back and allowed Diane to walk through into the hall.

'Mrs Craig asleep?' Diane asked.

Alison nodded. Thank heaven her mother had been asleep when she returned. The new doctor had given her a sleeping-pill and had said she would not wake before morning. It had meant that Alison could join Michael at the flat without need of concern for her mother. She had been so relieved, so excited at the thought of joining Michael. The new doctor had told her after his examination that he couldn't find anything wrong; had said that if Alison was really worried, he could take Mrs Craig into the new hospital under obser-vation for a week or two as soon as there was a free bed; but in his view, she was sound in mind and limb. Convinced now that Michael had been right all along, Alison had made up her mind finally not to let Mrs Craig rule her life any longer. When morning came she would have returned home to tell her mother that it was up to her to make her choice but that Alison was going to live with Michael.

But now, how could she ever live with him again?

'Look here, Alison, I know tonight was a bit of a shock for you. I can understand you hating me and I don't expect

159

any forgiveness for myself. But you must forgive poor Michael. We meant never to see each other again after your marriage. Of course, we'd have had to meet during the course of our work, but I mean – well, not intimately. Michael wasn't coming round to my flat any more. We were both quite resolved to be strong about it. I knew Michael was in love with you and I faced up to it. But I wasn't as strong as I'd thought – or Michael. One can't be just platonic when one is alone with someone with whom one has once had an affair.'

Alison listened, too horrified to interrupt. When Diane paused, she said weakly, 'But you both swore, that afternoon in your flat, that there was nothing between you!'

'What else could we do?' Diane replied, shrugging her shoulders. 'You're so frightfully innocent, Alison. You've no experience of the world and you believe that everyone can lead the same saintly life you do. If you'd known the truth then you would never have married Michael. And you can't really blame him. I was there and available, lonely and needing someone. Michael hadn't even met you when it all began. Well, we suited one another and saw each other as often as possible. The word began to get around that Michael was often at my flat late at night and we had to be more careful. Your mother heard about it and challenged me to tell the truth. Knowing then how Michael felt about you, I thought it best to be honest and admit it. But Michael didn't want you to know. He made me promise not to tell you. It was his marriage at stake, not mine, so what could I do? I had to lie to you.'

'So Mother knew the truth! She's been trying to protect me?'

'Yes, I suppose so!' Diane said as if admitting it unwillingly. 'Naturally, your mother's ideas are old-fashioned and she considers an affair dreadfully immoral. But surely you can understand, Alison!'

Alison drew in her breath sharply. Could she? Or was she just as old-fashioned as her mother? Did people nowadays go round making love whenever they felt like it? If so, she couldn't accept it for herself. What Michael had done in the past – yes, perhaps she could forget that. It didn't really touch on her, reflect on his love for her. But to have gone on seeing Diane, making love to her. No, it was horrible, horrible.

'I'm afraid we don't see life the same way,' she said to Diane coldly. 'I think it is unforgivable, Diane. It would have been bad enough before our marriage, but now – Michael is my husband. It's too horrible to think about.'

Diane stood up, sighing. 'Michael said it wouldn't be any good coming. I know he's intending to come and explain himself in the morning. He still loves you, Alison!'

'Loves me? And wants you!' Alison cried with a shiver. 'No, thank you, Diane. I don't share the man I love with anyone. You can keep him, and if you're going back to spend the night with him you can tell him from me I never want to see him again. Now get out of my house!'

'I'm sorry!' Diane said. 'I really am sorry!'

Alison did not reply, but pulled open the door and watched Diane walk quickly out into the rain.

It's over, finished! she thought wildly. For a few minutes she was too shocked, too numbed to feel any pain. Nothing was real, nothing made sense any more. Diane had gone, back to Michael. Soon they would be lying in each other's arms . . .

'No!' she cried aloud with sudden searing pain in her heart. 'No, no, no!'

But there was no one there to hear her cry.

161

Fifteen

Sunday morning and Michael awoke with a splitting headache. He looked round the bedroom, seeing the unfamiliar objects and strange furniture. He was neither in his digs nor in the hotel where he and Alison were honeymooning – Alison!

The thought of her brought back all that had happened. This was their home, he was lying in the big double bed they had been going to share. Alison...

He heard the clink of teacups and footsteps approaching the bedroom door. Could it mean Alison had come back last night? If only he could think more clearly, remember exactly what had happened.

The door opened and Diane came in, carrying a breakfast-tray. She looked poised and was carefully made up. There was a faint anticipatory smile on her face.

'Coffee!' she announced. 'Hot and black!'

Michael struggled into a sitting position and did not attempt to conceal the disappointment and surprise on his face.

'What are you doing here?' he asked. 'What time is it?'

'Nine A.M. And I'm here to look after your needs. You must have a pretty big hangover, Michael. I thought you'd like coffee first and something to eat afterwards.'

'Thanks!' Michael forced himself to say. 'It's decent of you to turn out so early.'

'Oh, I haven't come from my flat,' Diane corrected him, 'I've been here all night, Michael. Surely you realized that?'

Michael shook his head, trying to remember. But he could not. His last memory was of Alison's stricken face and the door closing behind her as she walked out of the flat.

162

'Alison . . .?'

Diane handed him his coffee and sat down on the edge of the bed, taking her own cup in her long white hands.

'I'm terribly sorry, Michael. I'm afraid she went back to her mother.'

'Damn it!' Michael said, nearly spilling his coffee as he jerked upright. 'I shall go round there straight after breakfast and bring her home. Time I took a firm stand.'

Diane said nothing, made no mention of her own visit to Alison after Michael had gone to bed. Let Michael say what he wished to Alison. It was doubtful she would listen to him, or believe him now. A faint smile played about her lips.

'Coffee all right?' she asked solicitously.

'Fine!' Michael said. 'Wish my head felt less heavy though. Diane, what *did* go on last night? I'm sure you shouldn't be here. If Alison knew, she'd think all kinds of things. So would anyone else, come to that!'

'Don't you remember?' Diane asked innocently. 'You decided the best way to bring Alison to her senses was to make her jealous. When she arrived, we were making love.'

She was not sure how much Michael remembered. If he really had been drunk at the time, perhaps he would believe that there had been more than a kiss.

'Making love!' Michael repeated, horrified. He recalled Diane's face close to his own – yes, and kissing her. But . . . 'Diane, you've got to tell me. We didn't . . . I didn't—'

'Stop worrying, Mike!' she said softly. 'Anything you did was all right by me. I know you don't love me and I know you want Alison back – if she'll come. But I'd like you to know that if she won't – well, I'm here if you need me.'

Michael put down his coffee cup and lay back against the pillow. There was an unreal quality about this conversation which made him wonder if he was still asleep, dreaming. What had really happened? What was Diane saying? What had he done to her to make her talk this way. He was sure he'd done no more than kiss her.

'I've got to get up,' he said abruptly. 'I must go and see Alison.'

'But your breakfast . . .' Diane began to argue. Michael waved it aside, unaware of her anger and frustration.

'Off you go, Diane, there's a good girl. We'll talk this out later. I must see Alison first.'

A cold fury stiffened Diane's back as she walked out of the room. It was obvious Michael had no interest in her – no desire to leave the warmth of Alison's arms for her own. Well, he would be forced to think again soon. Then, when he turned to her . . .

She never once doubted that he would and, with iron self-control, she hid her anger and gave Michael his head. Patience, she counselled her impatient heart. Your time will come.

Michael cut himself twice whilst shaving and swore loudly. He felt terrible and Diane's suggestion that there might have been more to last night than a mere kiss or two worried him desperately. He remembered now the plan to make Alison jealous, but he was sure it was Diane's idea and not his. Whoever it was, the plan had clearly worked. But would Alison believe him when he told her it was all a put-up job? How was he to explain Diane being here all night?

He got out his car and drove with a steadily rising depression to Alison's home.

To his complete and utter astonishment, it was Mrs Craig who answered the door when he rang the bell. Mrs Craig, fully dressed and up and about. Michael realized with a shock that this was the first time he'd seen her up.

'Well?' the older woman asked. She had been prepared for this. When Alison had told her this morning what had happened, she guessed Michael would be round to try to explain away his dastardly behaviour. Well, Alison should be protected, even if she had to get out of her sick-bed to do it. Firmly, she forced Alison back to bed, brought her a hot-water bottle, even brought her up some breakfast which a white-faced, tearful Alison refused to eat.

'Could I see Alison?' Michael asked tentatively, and then, realizing the absurdity of this remark: 'I wish to see my wife!'

'Alison is in bed and told me to tell you she has no wish to see you,' Mrs Craig stated firmly.

Michael felt suddenly furiously angry.

'Get out of my way!' he said, pushing her roughly to one side. He had a foothold now and she could not close the door in his face.

'This is my house!' Mrs Craig cried shrilly. 'You get out or I'll call the police!'

'Mother, don't!'

Alison stood at the top of the stairs, her face white and tear-streaked, her dressing-gown clutched firmly round her.

Michael bounded up the stairs but she shrank away from him.

'Alison, please! You've got to let me explain.'

'I don't want any explanations, Michael. I could never forgive you, *never*. It's all over. I never want to see you again.'

'Alison!' His cry went straight to her heart and she knew that, despite everything, she still loved him, still wanted him. But she wouldn't go back to him . . . never, never! 'Alison, you've got to listen. It was all a put-up job. I wanted to make you jealous. You've got to believe me!'

'I'm sorry, Michael. I don't. I don't trust you and I couldn't live without trust. What you can do once, you can do again and again. That isn't my idea of love – or marriage. You've lied and cheated ever since you first met me.'

Michael listened aghast. 'That's not true!' he shouted. 'I've never done a single thing you could object to until last night, and that was deliberately to shake you into some sense. You're hysterical, Alison.'

Alison shivered.

'You're very convincing, Michael, when you lie. But this time I happen to know the truth. Go back to Diane. She loves you. Why didn't you marry her in the first place? At least that would have been the decent thing to do.'

'You've been listening to your mother's lies about me!' Michael cried. 'She's poisoned your mind against me. Don't listen to her, Alison. I love you; I've never cared two

165

twopenny damns about Diane. You must believe that!'

'Then it's all the more shame on you to behave the way you do with her. We don't think along the same lines, Michael. I'm just not your type. I don't believe in free love when the fancy takes you. Obviously you do and so does Diane. I'll divorce you and then you can marry her.'

'I don't want to marry her. I don't want a divorce!' Michael shouted. 'Can't you understand, I'm in love with you. It isn't I who have cheated, Alison. It's you. You've never really belonged to me; half of you has gone on belonging to your mother. I thought if I gave you a chance you'd see she was tricking you, spoiling your life and my life. That didn't work and I was desperate. It seemed a good idea to make you think I did care about Diane. But it isn't true – it never has been. I swear it!'

'And you'd swear you've never slept with her? Made love to her?' Alison asked quietly.

Michael hesitated. It was only for the fraction of a second while he tried to remember last night, and then he knew with a deep inner certainty that nothing had happened except that kiss – Diane kissing him.

'Yes, I swear it!' he said. But it was too late. Alison had heard that second of silence and mistook it for a hesitation to lie to her again.

'I'm sorry, Michael. I can't believe you. I prefer to take Diane's word. She may be immoral but at least she was honest about it.'

'Diane's word?' Michael said frowning. 'You mean you believe that mother of yours before you believe me?'

Knowing nothing of Diane's visit, he assumed Alison to be reverting to the other occasion when his mother-in-law had lied about him.

'My God, Alison, look at her! Up and about and no signs of being a dying woman. I was right all along. She was shamming to keep you away from me. Now she's succeeded it doesn't suit her to be ill any more. She's tricked you once, Alison. Don't let her do it again.'

'It is you who have tricked me,' Alison cried passionately.

166

'Don't touch me, Michael. I couldn't bear it. Please go!'

His hands fell to his sides and he looked suddenly lost and helpless. Mrs Craig had won. Alison's mind had been poisoned against him.

He walked slowly downstairs and faced the woman who had done her best to ruin his life and had already succeeded in ruining his marriage.

He saw her contented, satisfied face and for a moment he wanted to hit her.

'You!' he shouted at her. 'You are responsible for this. And to think I was prepared to give you a home – to like you even, for Alison's sake. I have never felt so much hatred for any human being in my life.'

He pushed past her and went out of the house. There was a hard lump in his throat, a painful ache of misery which would get worse. He'd lost her . . . lost Alison, his wife.

Blindly, he got into his car and drove away. Without thinking, he steered a course to the surgery. He wasn't due back to work until tomorrow, but now he was here he knew he wanted badly to see Dr McFaddon. Maybe he could help, see Alison, talk some sense into her. Maybe all wasn't lost yet. It couldn't be! He wouldn't give up so easily.

'Great Scott, Michael!' Dr McFaddon greeted him. 'You look ghastly. What's happened?'

As briefly as possible, in a quiet, dead voice, Michael told him everything. Dr McFaddon heard him out and then took a deep breath.

'Something fishy going on, my boy. I don't like it. Too many lies. It just doesn't make sense. If ever I saw a girl madly in love it's Alison Craig the day she married you. Love doesn't die so easily. There's more to this than meets the eye.'

'But what?' Michael asked desperately. 'She believes all these lies her mother has told her about me. She takes her mother's word against mine. Yet you say she loves me. My God, if I weren't a doctor with a reputation to consider, I'd sue that woman for libel and clear my name.'

167

'Something wrong somewhere!' Dr McFaddon murmured again. 'I thought so when Mrs Craig told me she'd decided to change her doctor. Frankly, she's always been such a tiresome patient, I really didn't mind a lot. I was annoyed the way she cancelled that X-ray and I didn't stop to ask for reasons. Now a woman like that doesn't chop and change around; not after all these years. It wasn't you who spoke against me, nor Alison, who phoned me yesterday to say how sorry she was. So who was it? The only person who has been near her is Nurse Fellows. I wonder—'

'Diane!' Michael said. 'But why should she want to do that? She told me herself she'd tried everything to dissuade Mrs Craig from leaving you.'

'Yes, yes! But someone is lying. I'm going to get to the bottom of this, Michael. I don't like it – not at all.'

Michael ran his hand through his hair. 'I don't believe Diane had a thing to do with all this. She's been on our side. But for her Alison and I wouldn't have had a honeymoon. She's a good sort, Doc, and she has been a good friend.'

'Yes, well, I'm going to see Alison. I'm still *her* doctor and that old battleaxe can't keep me out.'

'Thanks!' Michael said gratefully. 'It's nice of you to bother. It's all a bit beyond me now. I just don't know what to do.'

'You go on home and get some sleep. You look as if you need it,' Dr McFaddon said with a smile.

'Afraid it's a bit of a hangover!' Michael said sheepishly. 'Diane kept giving me brandies—' He broke off, realizing as he spoke that here was Diane in the picture again. But for her, he certainly wouldn't have had more than a whisky before his meal.

'She may be there, at the flat!' he said quietly.

'Then send her home. Don't say anything to her about having talked to me. Tell her you'll see her later on.'

Diane was pacing the floor, to and fro, to and fro, waiting for Michael's return. When she heard his car draw up, she ran to the window and looked down. Her heart was beating furiously. This was the moment; soon she would know if

168

her plan had succeeded. No, Alison wasn't with him. She'd won . . . *won*!

'I'm feeling pretty ghastly!' Michael announced as he came into the room. 'I'm going to lie down for a bit. You push off home, Diane. I'll see you later on when I've slept off this hangover.'

It wasn't somehow quite what she had expected him to say. Uncertainly, she asked: 'Alison? She . . . you and she—?'

'It's stalemate!' Michael said. 'Alison seems to think you and I have been having an affair and won't consider coming back to me. But I won't give up hope!'

She sensed a reserve in his tone of voice and was for once quite unsure of herself. Should she be solicitous? Should she console him? Dare she place a sympathetic hand on his arm? She wanted desperately to touch him. Last night, in his arms, she had known all too surely how magnificent love between them could be. Then that confounded girl had walked in and she'd been left in mid-air, tasting but still not knowing the completion of love.

She gave a nervous little laugh. 'Almost makes one feel one might as well be hung for a sheep as for a lamb!' she said. 'You know, I am fond of you, Michael. You like me, too, don't you?'

He looked down at her consideringly. Could this friendly, quiet girl really have been working against him? Was the friendship only a blind? Did she really want something else?

'You're a very attractive woman, Diane!' he said quietly.

The answer pleased her. Michael did find her attractive.

'Sure you wouldn't like me to stay here with you?'

'No!' The rejection was instantaneous and complete. Her lips tightened in disappointment and anger. Soon the time would come when it was he who begged and she who had the power to refuse. Her love for him, or her obsession with him, was tinged now with a sadistic desire to hurt him. Hell hath no fury like a woman scorned! No, he would pay, but pay in the coin of passion. She'd make him want her so much he would be weak with desire. Then she would do with him as she pleased.

169

'See you later!' she said lightly. 'Come around to my place about six. We'll have a drink and chew it all over.'

She picked up her coat and went out, leaving him alone.

Dr McFaddon sat on the edge of Alison's bed and looked down at the young girl with pity. Tears had swollen her eyes and crying had made her voice hoarse.

'You do still love him?' he asked gently, knowing the question was unnecessary.

'Yes, of course! That's one of the awful things I keep thinking about. I ought not to go on loving someone who has lied and cheated. I despise him, yet I can't help loving him. We were so happy on our honeymoon—'

Her voice broke and Dr McFaddon patted her hand. 'I think your woman's instinct is more to be trusted than your reason,' he said. 'I know Michael pretty well. I know him well enough to be quite, quite sure that he would never have carried on an affair with anyone behind your back. It doesn't make sense, Alison. He didn't *need* anyone else once he had you. It's you he loves, he's told me over and over again.'

'But he wants her, too!' Alison said with a shiver. 'I've read that men can be like that. They can't help being attracted and it isn't supposed to affect their love for their wives when they are unfaithful. But it affects my love for him. If it were just once – but it's been going on for ages.'

'That's absurd!' Dr McFaddon argued. 'Do you think I wouldn't have known it if they had been having an affair? Why, Michael hardly noticed her on duty. It's only since he's known you that he became at all friendly with her. Then I think it was because he felt sorry for her.'

'They have tricked you in the same way as they deceived me,' Alison cried bitterly. 'I thought Diane was my friend. All the time, she and Michael . . . I can't bear to think about it.'

'But who told you they'd been having an affair?' the old man insisted. 'Your mother? You've got to face facts about her, Alison, for your own sake as much as Michael's. He was quite right about her. I saw her downstairs just now,

170

right as rain. A sick woman couldn't get up out of her bed and start running her house as if it were the normal everyday thing to do. I'm quite sure she's been out of her bed and on her feet whenever there's been no one around to see her.'

Alison bit her lip. It was true that her mother had made the most remarkable 'recovery'.

'Now admit it, Alison. I know it isn't very nice to think of, but it's true none the less.'

'I . . . I suppose so!' Alison admitted.

'Very well then. You'll admit also that she was dead set against Michael from the first and determined you should never marry him. It's not so hard to believe that she has fabricated these stories about him, too.'

'But it isn't *just* what Mother said!' Alison cried. '*Diane has admitted everything*. She came here last night and confessed. At least she was honest.' Her mouth twisted in bitterness. 'Michael denied it all this morning. It was horrible, standing there hearing him lie and lie.'

'You don't think Michael might be telling the truth and that it is Nurse Fellows who is lying?'

'Diane? But why? Why should she?'

'For the same reason your mother has. She wants you and Michael apart. It's my belief she wants Michael herself. I think she has been egging your mother on to do all she can to get you back. She had no right to telephone you while you were on your honeymoon. I'd told her myself I didn't think there was a thing the matter with your mother and that the X-ray was only a precautionary measure, more to keep her quiet than anything else. She asked me then if she should ring you and I said no. Now why should she want to spoil your honeymoon? She must have known you'd come back if she made your mother out to be ill enough.'

'No, no!' Alison whispered. 'That's horrible!'

'Yes, it is!' Dr McFaddon said sternly. 'And I've only just realized what has been going on. She's in love with Michael and she thinks if she can ruin your marriage, he'll turn to her.'

'But Diane isn't like that, I'm sure she isn't!' Alison found

171

herself arguing in Diane's defence. 'You told me yourself how devotedly she nursed her husband when he was dying. A woman like that couldn't—'

'A normal woman, no! But I don't think Nurse Fellows is normal. Not now, anyway. Michael told you she tried to kill herself? That may have been a neurotic way of drawing attention to herself. There are some women, Alison, who'll do anything, however humiliating or exacting or unscrupulous, to get the man they want.'

Alison shivered.

'I'm sure you're wrong. She's so quiet and poised and self-controlled.'

'On the surface, yes! Neither you nor I know what goes on beneath. People like your mother, Alison, are never dangerous. They are extroverts who pour out their woes and troubles and complaints. You know where you are with them. It's the quiet ones, the introverts who shut everything up inside, whom one should worry about. Michael, if he hadn't been so close to her, might have understood. He's the psychiatrist, not me. But you can't live to my years without getting some knowledge of people and types. That's why I'd back Michael to the last ditch. I think you should too, Alison.'

'I need time to think this out!' Alison said shakily. 'I want so much to believe you. But . . . well, I saw them together myself. Even if she was trying to . . . to make him unfaithful, surely Michael need not be so weak as to give way?'

'My dear, he told me himself this morning that it was Diane's idea that they should be kissing when you came to the flat. It was to make you jealous. Michael was desperate. He thought he was going to lose you. He was willing to try anything – and he'd had too much to drink.'

'He knew he wouldn't lose me. I loved him!' Alison cried.

'But not enough to stay out the rest of your honeymoon. Not enough to be there at the flat to greet him after a long lonely drive north to be reunited with you.'

'I would have been there!' Alison tried to defend herself. 'I was going, only Mother had fixed to see the new doctor at six and Diane said—'

172

'Well, what did she say?'

'She said Michael would never make the trip in twelve hours. He'd have to stop for lunch and in his old car it would take nearer fourteen. She said she'd go round and get the fires lit and the meal cooked and that if I turned up about eight, I'd be in plenty of time to greet him.'

'Michael says he was so anxious to see you, he didn't stop for lunch or tea. He drove as fast as he could and he reached the flat at ten past six. That gave her two hours alone with him, two hours in which to make it clear to him that you'd really preferred to stay with your mother; that he must do something drastic if he wanted you back. Very clever, Alison!'

'If anyone else but you had said this, I'd have thought them crazy. Do you really believe it, Dr McFaddon? You're not just saying this because you are sorry for Michael?'

'I can't prove it, Alison. Only you can do that. Go back to him, make Diane realize she has lost, not just this one round, but for always. Then, maybe, we'll see her in her true colours.'

'I don't know that I want to!' Alison said, shivering once more. 'It's so horrible. And Michael will never forgive me for doubting him.'

'He'd forgive you anything, Alison, so long as he is sure you love him. But you'll have to convince him of that. I think you'll have to make your choice once and for all . . . Michael or Mother.'

Alison gave a wry smile. 'I'm afraid he is right about Mother. But don't say anything to her yet, Dr McFaddon. She's so happy to think she has me home, and it's such a relief to see her well and about the house again. I'd like her to go on believing for a little while.'

'That's up to you, my dear. But don't leave Michael in despair too long.'

After he had gone, Alison lay on her bed, dry-eyed and thoughtful. Dr McFaddon had given her no proof. All he had told her was guesswork, and yet somehow deep down within her she knew it was true. It was like the missing piece of a jigsaw falling into place and making the whole picture complete. Diane, in love with Michael; prepared to go to any lengths to get him. How would she behave when she knew that her plan had failed?

Quite suddenly Alison hoped that Dr McFaddon was wrong. She no longer believed Michael had been unfaithful to her – perhaps she had never really believed it since she had gone on loving him! – but she didn't want to believe Diane was bad . . . really bad. And would Michael believe it?

Her mother came up with a cup of tea. Mrs Craig was like a mother-hen fussing round her young. Knowing that she had to disillusion her, Alison felt an ache in her heart. Poor Mother! But she would get over it. She must, because no matter what happened, she would never leave Michael again.

'How are you feeling, darling?'

'Much better! I'm going to stay here till lunch and then I shall get up and go for a walk.'

'Ought you to?' Mrs Craig asked anxiously. 'I'm sure you need a good long rest, dear.'

'I'm all right!' Alison said firmly. 'Don't worry about me, Mother.'

After lunch, she bathed her face, made up with care and put on the blue dress she knew Michael liked best. She felt nervous and excited and almost as if she were going to meet him for the first time. As she walked towards the flat, she prayed furiously that Michael would be there. The last doubt had gone. A morning of steady, clear thinking had convinced her that Dr McFaddon was right. She no longer doubted him.

She opened the door with her own key and felt a moment's disappointment. The sitting-room was empty. Then she heard Michael's voice from the bedroom, 'That you, Doc?'

She opened the door and saw him, lying on the bed. His face broke into a surprised and radiantly happy smile as he caught sight of her.

He sprang off the bed and a moment later their arms were round each other.

174

'Darling, darling!' Michael whispered. 'I never thought you'd come. I didn't dare hope it could be you. Oh, Alison ...my dearest love!'

She was crying unashamedly but smiling too. 'Forgive me!' she whispered. 'Forgive me!'

'As if there were anything to forgive!' Michael cried, wiping away her tears and kissing her wet cheeks and then her soft mouth. 'Oh, Alison, I feel as if we've been parted for years and not just four days.'

'Michael, I . . . I love you. I'll never leave you again.'

He looked at her with eyes that shone with content. 'I'll never *let* you go again!' he vowed.

He lifted her into his arms and carried her to the bed. To Alison, it was like the first night of their honeymoon, only somehow sweeter and more important. Then there had been love and desire and excitement, and Michael leading her, showing her the way. Now she needed no guidance but could love him on equal terms, their love all the deeper for having been so nearly lost.

Outside, the rain fell in a steady damp sheet, but inside their world was golden and warm and only the two of them existed, lost in love.

Sixteen

Dr McFaddon knocked on the door of Diane's flat and waited patiently. The rain had poured down, soaking him so that he felt old and tired and wished he could be anywhere else in the world but here.

Presently, the door opened and the expectant look was wiped off the girl's face as she saw who stood there.

'Oh, it's you!' she said, unguarded in her disappointment. It was past six and she had thought that Michael. . . 'Anything wrong, Doctor?'

'No, not really. But I'd like to come up for a few minutes if I may?'

Diane bit her lip. 'Well, it isn't awfully convenient just now. I am expecting someone. Would tomorrow—?'

'Michael won't be coming!' Dr McFaddon said sharply. He knew his guess had been right when he saw the look of unshaded venom she shot at him.

'How do you know?'

'If I may come in, I will explain.'

Diane stood back and allowed him to precede her into the sitting-room. The fire was glowing warm and the room was a pink glow of light. On the coffee-table stood a tray of drinks. Everywhere was the smell of Diane's perfume. It was an inviting, seductive, tempting room. Old as he was, Dr McFaddon sensed that this was a room prepared by a woman to receive the man she loves.

Diane, too, looked inviting, seductive and tempting. The long flimsy negligee clung to her figure, outlining the young beauty, the perfect curves. All of her was soft and rounded and warm, except her eyes. They glittered with a hard light, like diamonds.

176

'Well? You have a message for me?'

'No, Diane. No one sent me. I decided to come of my own accord. You see, I thought you might be interested to hear that Michael and Alison have been reunited. I don't think they will let anyone part them again.'

Diane's face crumpled slowly as she took in what he was saying. Disappointment beyond description was so acute that she could not pretend she didn't care. Her mouth twisted. After months of iron self-control, she was suddenly defenceless.

'Together? But it was over, finished. I don't believe it!'

He knew then that he'd been right. He knew, too, that it was as well he, a doctor, had come here this evening. This woman was not just evil – she was mentally unwell. He'd seen faces like hers before in hospital. He felt suddenly deeply sorry for her. What she had done was unforgivable; but she was not altogether responsible for her actions.

'You'll have to face it, Diane! He loves her and she loves him. He'll never come to you.'

'Won't he?' The sneer was terrible to hear and see. 'I'll make him. He's mine, do you hear? I've always wanted him. He's not weak like that fool I married. He's strong and beautiful and I need him!'

She went over to the old man and knelt at his feet, staring up at him from agonized eyes.

'Do you know what it is like to want a man and not have him? Do you know how many days and nights I've been tortured by the thought of him wasting his love on that idiot of a girl he married? She can't give him what I could give him. He'll see that. Once he has made love to me, he'll never want any other woman.'

'He'll never make love to you, Diane.'

She stood up, her face distorted in grief and rage. 'And what do you know about it, you silly old fool? Nothing, nothing! I tell you he is mine! I'll have him even if I have to kill her first! You don't believe me? I could do it. I will do it rather than lose Michael!'

'I believe you, Diane. I think you could do it. Tell me,

177

weren't you ever in love with your own husband?'

Diane stood up and walked to the window. 'In love with Peter? If I'd had the courage I'd have seen him dead a lot sooner than Fate intended. No, I despised him. I want no weakling for a mate. I want a man like Michael; and I'll have him, do you hear? I've waited a long time. I've been very patient. You don't know how long the days and nights have been – especially the nights.' Her voice changed suddenly to a thin whine. 'It wouldn't be fair, would it? After I've waited so long. Michael couldn't be so cruel. I knows he likes me . . . he finds me attractive. Don't you think I'm attractive, Doctor?'

She looked at him provocatively and he had a hard job to remind himself that this was the same cool, poised young woman who helped him in the surgery. He felt sickened and at the same time his horror was softened by the intense pity he always felt for anyone mentally unbalanced.

She'd have to go into hospital for treatment. Maybe in time she would get better and be able to lead a normal life again. But what she had said about her first husband made him doubtful. If it were true that she had only pretended to love him yet secretly despised him and was glad when he died, then it looked as if she had been unbalanced, to say the least, all that time ago.

Her voice was now angry, demanding an answer from him, the reassurance he could not give.

'My dear, I'm sorry, but Michael is now completely reconciled with Alison. It's hard for you but you must try to accept it.'

'Never, never!' Diane spat the words at him. Her eyes narrowed and she gave a quick high-pitched laugh. 'I'll think of some way to get rid of her. You'll help me, won't you? Maybe there's something we could give her – something to make her very ill. You'll help me, won't you, Doctor? You believe Michael belongs to me . . . that she's stolen what is mine?'

Dr McFaddon stood up, feeling very old and tired. He knew he must handle her now with the greatest tact.

178

'I want to help you, Diane!' he said quietly. 'I know you will agree it is always difficult to think clearly when you are overwrought. I'd like you to let me give you something to soothe your nerves. It will help to clear your mind and then we'll plan the future.'

She was suddenly happy to think she had an ally. She quickly rolled up her sleeve and laid her bare arm before him.

'I'm not afraid of injections. I used to have lots when I was young. I used to get over-excited and they gave me injections to make me calm.'

Dr McFaddon helped her gently into a chair then opened his small black bag and took out the syringe, filling it with care. A moment later, he had plunged it into her arm.

Already she was getting drowsy. She looked at him from trusting half-closed eyes. The evil had left them now. There was something childish in their expression.

'I'm not so easily beaten, am I?' she asked sleepily. 'In the end I always get what I want.'

The moment she was asleep, the old doctor phoned for an ambulance. He went with her to the hospital and saw the doctor in charge of the psychiatric ward, explaining her case to him. Diane had already been taken up to the ward and put to bed by the time he got into his car to drive home. He knew that he would be unlikely to see her again. Perhaps none of them would.

Not many minutes later he was sitting by the fire in Michael's flat. Both young people looked grave as he told them the result of his visit to Diane. Alison clung to Michael's hand, her face frozen with horror and pity.

'But we never guessed – none of us guessed!' she said at last.

'No, darling,' Michael said gently. 'But it wouldn't have helped her much even if we had known, although it would have saved us a great deal of heartache.'

'Poor Diane, poor Diane!' Alison said repeatedly.

'There's a great deal modern science can do now for mental cases,' old Dr McFaddon tried to comfort her. 'Now I think it is best if you both forget her if you can. She meant only evil to you both and you should not pity her too much. You know, Alison, but for you Michael might have fallen into her trap, and then what kind of wife would he have had?'

'Marry Diane? I never once thought of it!' Michael cried, so indignantly that both Alison and the old doctor laughed.

After Dr McFaddon had gone Michael put his arms round his wife and held her close against him. 'Don't be too upset, my darling! No one is to blame and we can only be thankful that she didn't do any worse harm than trying to put effect to her plans. Of course, your mother must be told. I'm afraid it will be a nasty shock for her.'

'I'm afraid it will!' Alison agreed and sighed. 'Maybe Mother needs a few shocks. I've yet to tell her that I'm never leaving you again, Michael. She'll be so worried. Won't you come home with me? Maybe we could tell her together about Diane. Mother isn't really bad, you know, in herself!'

'As if *your* mother could be bad!' Michael said tenderly. 'Yes, I'll come, darling.'

Together they drove to Alison's home where Mrs Craig was anxiously awaiting her daughter. She did not tell either of them that Dr McFaddon had already called on her. At first she had been too shocked to realize the implications of what he had said. But gradually, as he pointed out the facts, she knew that Diane had been using her as a pawn to gain her own ends. She was forced to realize that she really had nothing at all against Michael except that her daughter loved him.

'You don't want to ruin their lives, I know,' old Dr McFaddon had said gently. 'You acted as you did thinking it to be for Alison's good. But now you know the truth. He's a good boy, steady, devoted, reliable and a first-rate doctor. Try to see him in a fresh light. They both are willing to have you live with them and I think it is a fine idea. There are so many ways in which you can make life easier for them both. Think it over, Mrs Craig. You know, you might have had a son-in-law who was quite unwilling to forget the many insults you have slung at that lad!'

180

It was over an hour since he had left her. Alone she had thought over all he had said and she was suddenly deeply ashamed of the way she had behaved. It was no excuse to tell herself that but for Diane she would never have done those things. She ought to have been sufficiently strong-minded to run her own life.

As the minutes ticked by, she grew suddenly terribly afraid. Suppose Alison and Michael had decided not to bother with her any more? Suppose, after all, they were unwilling to forgive her? Suppose they didn't want her in their home now? It would be no less than she deserved, but she couldn't bear it.

Tears of relief sprang to her eyes as she heard the car draw up at the gate, heard two sets of footsteps on the path. As the door opened and they came in, hand in hand, the tears welled over and splashed down her cheeks.

It was Michael, not Alison who took her in his arms; Michael who patted her shoulder and said:

'Now, Mum, you can't do that there 'ere!' making them all smile, if a little shakily.

'Oh, Michael, Alison, my dears! Will you ever forgive a stupid, selfish old woman?' she asked.

'It's all forgiven and all forgotten . . . on one condition!' Michael said sternly.

Mrs Craig looked at him helplessly.

'The condition being that you let Alison help you pack your things *now*. You're coming right back home with us!'

She began to cry again, tears of relief. But even as she did so, she remembered the silent vow she had made never to be selfish again. She blew her nose and wiped her eyes.

'It's very sweet of you both, and I will come. But not today, not now. I spoilt your honeymoon and I want to be allowed to make up for it. You shall have a whole week alone with each other before I move in.'

'Oh, Mother!' Alison said, kissing her grey head gently.

'Nonsense. You come back with us now,' Michael insisted. But Mrs Craig was adamant.

'I'm a silly old woman, Michael, and I don't like being rushed. Give me a week to sort out my things.'

He was not taken in by this excuse but accepted her desire to make amends. It would be nice to have a week alone with Alison in their flat, just the two of them. A kind of second honeymoon. Decent of the old girl. She wasn't going to be such a nuisance after all!

'Come, darling!' he said to Alison. 'Your mother is quite right. I know her generation hates being rushed into things. Your mother will be quite all right!'

Looking from one to the other, Alison felt strangely lost. It seemed they had reached some private understanding which she had not yet grasped. She frowned, and then, suddenly, smiled. A happy relationship between the two people dearest to her in the world was what she wanted most. It had finally happened and she must not interfere.

She kissed her mother tenderly and then, taking Michael's proffered hand, she followed him back to the car.

'Home!' he said softly as he climbed in beside her. 'Home, my darling wife.'